JG NOLAN was born and raised in a sleepy village in Shropshire and loved writing stories and playing football as a child.

He has been a teacher for many years, working mainly with children who have had difficult beginnings in life. He strongly believes in positive thinking and feels most things are achievable if you put your mind to it.

When his football mad son, Robbie, was much younger, he kept breaking bones and was told by the doctors that he should never play football again. It was during one of his many lengthy stays visiting Robbie in the local children's hospital that the idea for *Jump!* drifted into JG Nolan's mind.

JG Nolan began to read the exploits of famous, maverick footballers from the past, to inspire his son and give him hope. Whilst doing this, he became more and more drawn to the tales of famous Celtic legends from the 1920s, whose names are still chanted in Parkhead to this day. It soon became clear to him- his first book would have to be set in Scotland.

JG Nolan's research led him to discover the iconic, ethereal, Cathkin Park.

After meeting Scottish actor Simon Weir, who has helped preserve the park for many years, the pieces of the jigsaw fell into place and *Jump!* was born.

When JG Nolan's son started on his long road to recovery and fitness, his determination to succeed reached the ears of famous local footballer Joe Hart, then at Manchester City. Joe very kindly sent Robbie some signed goalkeeper gloves to cheer him up during treatment. Robbie would eventually follow in Joe's footsteps and attend the same secondary school in their home town, Shrewsbury. Years later, after Joe had transferred to Celtic, he was thrilled to be asked to read *Jump!* and offered to write the foreword. A truly serendipitous chain of events!

CARINA ROBERTS is an award-winning artist and illustrator who loves creating characters and telling stories. Carina spent her childhood drawing, reading and befriending animals – it was in these first few years that her dream to be an illustrator was born. She's been running with it ever since!

She specialises in creating books, particularly for young readers – a lot of her inspiration comes from the wilds of Wales where she lives. She adores fiction and nonfiction alike – after working on illustrations for the National Trust in 2020 she is especially keen that her work encourages more people to go on an adventure.

Website: https://carinarobertsillustration.co.uk/

Instagram: https://www.instagram.com/carinarobertsillustration/

Twitter: https://twitter.com/RobertstheRed

JUMP!

"Its never over..."

Written By

JG Nolan

Illustrated By

Carina Roberts

Produced By

Sian Bagci

SilverWood

Published in 2022 by SilverWood Books

SilverWood Books Ltd
14 Small Street, Bristol, BS1 1DE, United Kingdom
www.silverwoodbooks.co.uk

'Willie Maley': Original version written by David Cameron circa 1970
and in the public domain.
'Come on you Bhoys in Green': Unknown author/s and in the public domain.
'Hail! Hail! The Celts are here': Unknown author/s and in the public domain.

ISBN 978-1-80042-129-5 (paperback)
ISBN 978-1-80042-130-1 (ebook)

British Library Cataloguing in Publication Data
A CIP catalogue record for this book is available from the British Library

Page design and typesetting by SilverWood Books
For further information please visit www.sergarcreative.co.uk

For Rosanne, Alex and Robbie

"Dwell on the beauty of life. Watch the stars, and
see yourself running with them."
Marcus Aurelius

"The greatest glory in living lies not in never falling,
but in rising every time we fall."
Nelson Mandela

Foreword

In my 18 years as a professional footballer, playing on some serious stages all around the world, I know what it takes to make it. I believe you need passion, energy and most of all hard work. I think Robbie Blair brings all of these. And more.

Everyone has their own path in life. Robbie Blair certainly has his. I've had a solid career, I've had ups and I have had downs. But I've never lost touch with that kid who just wants to get out there and play football – even if others say you can't! We can all learn from Robbie Blair.

Joe Hart

Acknowledgements

Jump! could not have come into existence without the support and encouragement of family, friends, and strangers.

There are so many people to whom I am thankful to but here are just a few……

Firstly, thanks to my Dad, Cyril, for always believing in me as a writer and for providing invaluable insights into football from the last billion years!

Additional thanks go to Sian Bagci of Sergar Creative Ltd for producing *Jump!* and project managing this from a Word document to the beautiful, finished creation you are holding now! Lots of blood, sweat and tears went into stitching every part of this book together as well as organising me and the *Jump!* journey.

Huge thanks go to Rosanne for endlessly trawling through drafts, providing feedback and encouragement.

While writing Jump! many people were involved at various stages from research, fact checking, proofing, editing as well as those who read through early drafts. Their prompt feedback and unwavering encouragement really spurred me on, so thank you to my friends from Shrewsbury Squash Club especially Guy, Don, Ade, Charlie, and Alex and Robbie for your support and to Paul Fowler for his sage advice. Ryan Heath was also a great help with his many professional insights into the world of sport and fitness training.

Early guidance and wise advice from Hilary Jones proved instrumental in the decision to choose SilverWood Books to share this journey and publish *Jump!* Thank you.

I was lucky enough to be encouraged by valued friends who have walked this path before me – many thanks to Ted Eames, Peter Adams and Graeme Daniels for their insight and practical support.

I was also fortunate to receive encouragement and guidance from people who were strangers to me at the outset but selflessly took time to give me a few pointers into this new literary world – thank you Ian Cleverdon, Huw Powell and Malcolm Hollingdrake. I promise I will pay it forward if I am placed in the same position!

I always felt that the illustrations in *Jump!* would be a critical part of bringing the story to life and for that I am grateful to Carina Roberts for immediately 'getting it' and adding so much to our project and to Derek Seymour for capturing the character of the legendary Patsy Gallacher in his fantastic drawing. Additional thanks to Rob Dunsford for his technical support and guidance.

I loved researching all about Celtic FC, Patsy Gallacher and Clydebank and thoroughly enjoyed visiting! I was met with enthusiasm, humour and generosity from everyone I encountered in the Glasgow area, and I look forward to returning very soon.

Special thanks though to Fred Frisby for taking the time to tell me about his life in Clydebank.

There have been incredible moments of serendipity throughout this project where the stars have just aligned perfectly. A standout moment was meeting Simon Weir whose passion for Cathkin Park was infectious and who has continued to be a support and believer in the book ever since. Another standout moment was in August 2021 when this book was already in production and the news announced that Joe Hart had just signed for Celtic FC. As a fellow Shropshire lad being drawn to the green half of Glasgow, I felt that this was some sort of message from the footballing Gods! I was therefore delighted that not only did Joe read *Jump!* but he took the time to write the foreword!

Grateful thanks to both Robert Jones and Agnes Hunt Orthopaedic Hospital and The Birmingham Childrens Hospital for their expertise and care in the treatment of 'our' Robbie.

Finally, thanks to anyone who has shown any interest in the creation of this book. Writing a book is a lonely old process so any positivity or interest shown is vital, for me anyway!! The wave of support I received helped get the flippin' thing over the finishing line!

Many thanks to Helen Hart and all the team at SilverWood for all their support and guidance.

If you have enjoyed *Jump!* please mention it to your friends, family and to anyone you think will be interested. Word of mouth, feedback and social media noise will encourage more people to delve into the world of Robbie Blair and I need your support to make it happen – I have more books within me waiting to come out!!

Until next time,
JG Nolan

www.sergarcreative.co.uk

Chapter 1

The Sky

It was neither dark nor stormy. There was nothing in the sky. Nothing in the calm waters of the Clyde estuary that lay, uninterested, observing in the distance. It wasn't like it was in one of those old books that Robbie was still too young to read. Because this wasn't a book. This was real. And in real life there are no clues in the sky.

Robbie was not to know, as he walked onto the football pitch of Our Holy Redeemer's Primary School for his debut game, that he would break his femur for the third time. He was not to know, as he shook hands with the captain, as the referee blew the whistle, as the seagulls squawked high above him as they always did, that within minutes he would be taken to the ground with a bruising swipe to his thigh that would leave his leg shattered in two and finally end his dreams of being a footballer. He was not to know any of this until it happened. Because this was not a book.

Chapter 2

The Psychologist

'So how old are you, Robbie?' the man asked.
    'Eleven.'
    'And when did you first start feeling different?'
    'What d'you mean? I feel fine.'

The man scrunched up his face, took his glasses off and touched his forehead. Was this his thinking face? He glanced down at his notes and then forced a weak smile.
    'When did you first see the face?' The face. The face.

Chapter 3

It's Over

As he left the front door for school, his mum called out to him.

'See you later. At the game. I'm finishing early so I'll be there. Be careful. Don't do anything stupid. You know what the doctor said.'

'Yeah, yeah,' Robbie replied, ignoring her twice. He started walking. Then he quickened, as he imagined he was in the game, darting down the wing, past player after player. They were powerless against Robbie's pace and skill. By the time he reached the entrance to his school, he was in full flight, ready to receive the ball back, skip past the keeper and then…

'Hey, Robbie!' It was the caretaker, Stuart, who also helped to train the school team. 'Dunna wear yourself out, son. We need you today.'

'I'm good,' Robbie told him. And he was good. He was very good.

At 2pm the referee blew. The seagulls squawked above them. As they always did. At last. At last. Robbie's whole week had been about this game. It was this and nothing else. Nothing else mattered. It was almost too much. It was like he had been asleep for the previous six and a half days, only to be woken now for this moment. And now. And now was here.

The ball bounced around randomly for a few moments and then

gravitated towards Robbie. He killed it dead with some part of his body (he didn't know which) and then that was it.

The music played out in his mind. Robbie wasn't particularly into music but he could hear a song – the drums, the bass, a voice. It built up as he ran. He flew past the first defender, rainbow-flicked the next. And then they ran out of defenders. The song was deafening. He was through, one-on-one with the keeper. And then… Silence. Nothing. Because when you are one-on-one with a keeper, the music stops.

He looked the keeper in the eyes. The keeper stood there, making himself big. But not big enough. Robbie knew exactly what he was going to do, and drew back his foot. He looked like he was going to smash it right through the keeper, but at the last moment, as the keeper flinched, Robbie gently dinked it over his stretching, beaten hands. The ball took an eternity to reach the back of the net, but it did. Obviously.

Stuart looked at Mr McDougal.

'I told him to stop those bloody rainbow flicks. But hey…'

Mr McDougal stared into the distance.

'But he's good. That's it.'

It was 1-1. One all. A great score, in a way. No one's winning, no one's losing, all to play for. It isn't boring. And it wasn't boring.

Time was running out. The referee looked at his watch. Mr McDougal shook his head. Hamish played a through-ball to Scott, who turned his man in an instant and played it through to Robbie, who was waiting. Ready. Instead of going right, Robbie ran straight. Nothing else mattered. Then a defender appeared from nowhere. Robbie could see. He could always see. He saw Andy whizzing down the wing and pushed it out to him. Then he waited. The ball swirled into the penalty area and Robbie saw it in slow motion. It was like the moon.

It didn't hurt at first. But when it did… Like the worst pain imaginable. And faces, faces over him, a sea of faces.

*

They carried him. Apparently, the worst thing you could do. He found that out when he was older. But at the time it seemed like the right thing to do.

His mum rushed over to the scene.

She was upset, pale. 'I told you, Robbie. Never again. It's over!'

And they carried him. His crippled, skinny body cradled by his muddy teammates. The sky above. The seagulls.

Then the face.

It was craggy, like someone from a book.

'It's never over,' it said.

Chapter 4

The Shirt

One year before

'Children, today we are going to do something different,' said Mr McDougal.

'The Reverend is keen to de-clutter the church and get rid of items that have had their day. Considering we have been looking at money and real-world maths problems, I have suggested to the Reverend that we help him by setting up a car boot sale outside the church. Anything that looks ridiculously old, we'll obviously tell the Reverend and he can sell it on eBay or something similar. But all the rest we can deal with and can sell at the sale. Sifting through the chapters of history and making a wee profit for the church! What's no' to like?'

'And no lessons for two days! Cheers, sir,' said Hamish.

'Bet we still have to write up what we've done,' replied Robbie.

They lined up along South Bank Street outside Our Holy Redeemer Church. The children couldn't keep to a line and wiggled around, not seeing the elderly people walking past who had been to fetch their milk and newspapers. It was a normal day. Again. Robbie was looking forward to these two days. He was good at school and would always do well, but a day sifting through rubbish and a day selling it to people, instead of lessons – what was not to like?

The old wooden door creaked open.

'Welcome, children. May I firstly say thank you for coming here today. By helping me to de-clutter the church of unwanted items you are not only doing a good deed for me, you are also helping God. God bless you all.'

'Aye, and we also get to miss Maths,' said Hamish.

'Enough, Hamish!' shouted Mr McDougal.

Once in, the children were taken through the church to the vestry. 'Anything that looks very old or valuable, tell your teacher or myself and we will put it to one side. If it looks like rubbish, put it over here.'

Most of it was rubbish. Apart from dusty old objects and pictures of long-forgotten saints looking out from long-forgotten frames, most of what they found was rubbish. Framed posters advertising long-forgotten events, bits of foldable seats, unusable children's toys, unwanted books that were now wanted even less, and obscure rusty fittings that once fitted something somewhere.

Robbie was transfixed. He'd never been particularly into history at school. It was better than Maths; anything was better than Maths. The ancient Egyptians left him cold. Stonehenge was okay and meant a morning making monuments out of cereal packets. Vikings were better and he enjoyed dressing up as one, even if he forgot about it until 8pm the night before and his mum had to fashion something out of a car rug and an unwanted plastic bowl. But, pretty much, Robbie wasn't that bothered by the past. He liked playing football. Being on the pitch. Scoring goals. Not looking back – though he did track back and help the defenders if he felt they weren't putting a shift in.

After two hours, Mr McDougal announced, 'Children, we'll break for lunch in five minutes.'

'Thank goodness!' said Hamish. 'I'm bored now. It's all rubbish.'

'Wait a minute!' said Robbie. 'What's that?' Pulling back some discoloured plastic sheeting, Robbie noticed a large trunk. The trunk had a belt which surrounded it but was unattached. Removing the top of the trunk was easy, and they peered inside. It was full of clothes, old clothes. They smelt old, old and dusty and as they pulled the clothes out, the forgotten dust shone against the beams of sunlight that filled the vestry. Patterned blouses, scarves, old school socks. And then something they couldn't quite work out. It sort of looked like a shirt. But it didn't have a collar. It had buttons by the opening for the neck. It was white and had green hoops, like Celtic, but the hoops were narrower and there were more of them. Robbie felt the material between his fingers. It kind of felt woollen, but smoother. Not like a scarf. Stretching it out in front of him, he quickly realised it was his size.

'Try it on!' said Hamish.

'Nah!' said Robbie. 'I cannae. It'd feel weird!'

'Go on! I bet it'd fit.'

Robbie took off his school jumper and placed it on the crate. He pulled the jersey (and 'jersey' seemed to describe it nicely) over his head. As he did so, he felt a strange feeling, as if it was always meant to be, as if he had worn it before. When he pushed his skinny arms through the sleeves, they felt enclosed and at home – like it had been made for him.

'You look good,' said Hamish.

At this point the Reverend came in. 'Well, don't you look a picture, laddie?'

'What do you mean, Reverend?' said Robbie.

'That's yours,' said the Reverend.

'What d'you mean, Reverend?' Robbie repeated.

'That shirt is meant to be yours. It's no good to me. Have it.'

'Thanks,' Robbie said. He then folded the jersey and put it carefully in his rucksack before running off to join the others for lunch.

Chapter 5

The Hospital

It was grey and misty. It wasn't raining but it felt like it was. Maybe that's just Scotland.

They drifted through the double doors, rested in the corridor for a few minutes, then Robbie was moved into a room. He lay there in the starched sheets, frightened, pale and wet with sweat. The pain in his leg still surged through his body, and when the nurse asked him to rate it, he gave it a nine out of ten. Mrs Blair sat by his bed holding his hand.

'Here again, wee man!'

'Aye,' Robbie said, wincing with the pain. It was what he normally said, but it was actually all he could muster.

A nurse came into the room and gave Robbie some medication to take. She said it would help to take away the pain. Some more nurses shuffled in and out, taking the clipboard from the end of his bed and filling it in. New arrivals tended to receive a lot of action. Robbie Blair was no stranger to the Royal Hospital for Children, Glasgow. He had been here many times during his short life. Leg breaks were the worst. They took longer to heal, and there was the dreaded traction, which basically meant five to six weeks on your back. Though he had broken his femur twice before, the dreaded thought of five weeks on his back was unbearable. But, stirring, he suddenly remembered there was some hope. Yes, he remembered that last time he was here the doctor had told him that when children were about nine or ten they would be big enough to have their bones pinned – thus no traction, and a shorter time in hospital – like a week! This thought lifted him, and as he was ten – nearly eleven – it was surely what the doctor would tell him. With this thought filling his mind Robbie, exhausted from the extended second half of his day, fell into a sleep.

When he awoke, a dark-haired man with rolled-up sleeves and a stethoscope around his neck was looking at him.

'Hello, Robbie. So what have you been up to, young man?' he asked kindly.

'Playing football,' Robbie told him.

'We've looked at the X-ray, Robbie. You have a fractured femur.'

'I know,' Robbie told him. 'I know I have.'

'According to the notes, this is the third time for your femur. Ooh, and it's not the only bone you have broken, I see. Gosh, there's quite a list, Robbie.'

'Yes, doctor. He's no stranger to this hospital, I'm afraid,' said Mrs Blair.

'The femur is so hard to break. Almost impossible,' he sighed.

'I know,' Robbie said.

'As you know, Robbie, the normal course of treatment for a leg fracture is traction. At your age we would normally be looking to pin your bones,' he said, gesturing with his fingers.

'Aye,' Robbie nodded, brightening.

'But…'

What did he mean – 'but'? Robbie thought there could be no 'but'.

'But,' the doctor went on, 'due to your physical size – you're a wee lad, Robbie – we will probably opt for traction.'

Robbie groaned inside. His day was just getting worse.

His mum started talking about work and how she was going to combine it with the regular trips to the hospital. She let go of his hand and began an endless series of text messages to various work colleagues, employers and family members.

The doctor continued, 'Well, I'll let you get some more sleep, Robbie, and we'll be back in a while to set up the traction.'

Mrs Blair was outside the room with her phone. Robbie lay there. He peeled back his sheets and looked at his muddied broken leg, which seemed totally at odds with the sea of white that surrounded it. It was cold as he lay there, and the light had dropped. There seemed no colour at all in the room, as if it had been drained away. Robbie closed his eyes. The colour came back. In the distance he heard his mum talking to her boss. The door opened. Robbie felt a hand on his shoulder.

'You can do this!' came the voice.

Chapter 6

The Room

When Robbie woke, he assumed it was morning but couldn't be sure. He slowly moved his eyes around the room, also moving his head as he did so, his surroundings too unfamiliar as yet to cover in a quick glance. But this would change. Soon his eyes would know every inch of this small room, every blemish on the wall, every scratch on the window that lay to his left and stood between him and the world he had once again been taken from.

He looked again to his left and checked to see if his mum was there. No. But a foldable bed lay there in the tight space between his bed and the wall. The blankets and sheets were unmade and an open overnight bag sat in the middle. Just then the door opened and his mum walked through – her work clothes on, her hair wet from a shower.

'Hello,' she said. It was morning then, he thought.

'Right, wee man, here's what's happening,' Mrs Blair went on. She sounded like she was in a rush. She normally was. 'So I'm off to work now. Your Auntie Jackie is coming over to be with you at eleven, and she'll be with you till two. I should be here at about five, all being well. I've drawn up a rota. There should be someone with you most days. Do you want me to get you anything?'

'Dunno. Football magazine, maybe. Na, forget it. A comic? Sweets.'

'Aye, well, I'll see what I can do. Now, take care. I'll see you later.'

'Take care? I cannae do much from here!'

'Aye,' his mum said, tilting her hair forward. 'I know, love. Get some sleep. You spent most of the night talking. I don't know where you were.'

Kissing him, Mrs Blair quickly slipped away, off to face the next challenge of her day.

Robbie thought. His mum never mentioned his dad. Did he even know? Probably not. It had been so long since Robbie had seen his dad. But even when he was there, he wasn't really, Robbie thought. The best memory – sometimes the only memory – he had of his dad was playing football with him in some park in the southside of Glasgow when he was about four or five. They used to live there before they moved to Clydebank. Like a proper family then.

Then Robbie thought: he hadn't looked at his leg yet. He braced himself, opened his eyes and looked down. It lay there, bandaged now, stretched out on a metal traction plate, secure but hanging, if you like, from the pulley system that was attached to the end of his bed. When did they do that? Must have been when he was asleep.

And then the pain again, bursts of pain surging through his leg and up his body. Robbie reached out for the button that hung by his pillow, the button that alerted a nurse.

A nurse briskly entered the room. 'How are you, Robbie? Is it still hurting?'

'Aye,' Robbie said.

'I'll get something for it, Robbie. What would you say out of ten?'

'Eight. And a half,' Robbie replied, grimacing. 'Ouch – maybe nine.'

'Oh dear,' the nurse said. 'I won't be long.'

She was pretty. Slim, with dark straight hair pulled into a ponytail. As she checked the information on the clipboard that hung on the end of his bed, she spoke again. 'Have you slept much? You were talking a lot in your sleep. Well, shouting really. Were you reliving it?'

'I'm…I'm not sure. What was I saying?'

'Oh, let me think. You cried out for someone called Hamish to pass to you. Were you playing football, Robbie? When you did it?'

'Aye,' Robbie nodded. 'Hamish crossed it into me. I was about to score.'

She went on. 'An' then you cried out, "No, not again!" You broke your leg before, Robbie?'

'A few times, aye.'

'And then you shouted, "Who are you? Why are you here? Why are you helping me?" You sounded very confused, Robbie. Anyway, I'll go and get you your meds.'

Robbie lay back on his pillow and thought again about the game.

Chapter 7

The Window

In the morning Robbie was moved to the general ward. There were two other children on the ward. In front of him to his left was a young girl called Ruby, who needed corrective hip surgery. In front of him to his right was an older boy, who had a broken tibia. He had glasses and almost had a moustache.

As Robbie lay there reading his comic, he saw a lady walk into the ward. Every second seemed like a minute for most people. For Robbie Blair it seemed like a year. The lady walked towards the double window that stretched out to the side of Robbie's bed.

'Hello there! What have you been up to?'

'I broke my leg. I've broken loads of bones. I used to play football. But this is it. I cannae play football anymore.'

Turning her head to one side and looking at him pointedly, the lady replied, 'Well, never say never, dear. There're so many things they can do for you. The traction will help you on your way – it has done for a hundred years, since the First World War. And then there's the medicine and the water therapy. There's lots to help you. And best of all – stay positive! Never give up, Robbie.'

'Aye, maybe,' Robbie replied, not very positively.

The lady then turned her attention again to the window. 'So, young man! What will this window say?'

Robbie thought for a bit and then answered, 'I'm not sure. What are windows meant to say?'

The lady had a round face with friendly eyes. 'I've come to paint the windows, and I always ask the children to tell me what story you want the windows to tell.'

Robbie, on his back as always, eyes closing, day merging into night, became aware of the temperature dropping. Just at that moment his face dropped to the side and then juddered back to the centre and then to the side. Then it became light again. Was it morning? He couldn't tell. The lady from earlier appeared again. She started drawing again on the window. She had drawn that afternoon but now she was drawing again – for Robbie.

'What do you like?' she asked.

'Celtic. Football.'

'Okay,' she said, thinking. 'My husband is a Celtic fan. What shall we do? Shall we draw the current team? Who's your favourite player?'

Robbie thought for a moment. He felt too sleepy to answer even this most basic of questions.

'I cannae remember. Maybe we could have some older players too. My auntie brought me this book about Celtic in the old days.'

Robbie handed her the book, and the lady – Jo was her name – sat on the side of the bed. They read it together.

'Okay,' she said. 'If we're going old, let's go for it. What about this team? Let's make these players come to life, Robbie. Hello, Jimmy Quinn. Hello, James McGrory. Now, who's this? Hello, Patsy Gallacher.'

And so she went to work.

Robbie watched as she drew and painted on the nondescript hospital window, with its flaking frame and sill. Chalk figures, then watercolour, then pastel. Robbie watched dreamily as the story on the window unfolded, figure by figure, colour by colour. And as Robbie drifted off again the figures, which now looked real, began to call out to each other, to pass, to score goals once again.

Chapter 8

The Wheelchair

Three weeks later

There was a knock at the door.

'Maw! There's someone at the door.' Robbie was in the lounge watching television.

Mrs Blair opened the door. It was Hamish.

'Come in, won't you?' she said, showing Hamish through to the lounge and clearing magazines for him to sit down. 'Robbie, I'll leave you boys to it. I'm going out to Tesco's. I'll see you in a wee while,' she announced as she moved to the door.

The door shut, and the boys were left by themselves.

Hamish looked at Robbie, who still looked into the distance.

'What you been up to?'

'Nothing. Sitting here, sitting upstairs, sitting outside. Lots of sitting.'

'Okay. We've got a game later. Are you coming?'

'What's the point? Doctors say I'll nae play again, and I cannae even walk. What you gonna do? Wheel me on as a mascot?'

'Be good to have you there.' There was a pause. Hamish continued.

'And we miss you.'

'Thanks,' Robbie said, turning away.

Hamish got up. 'I've got to go. Sorry, Robbie. Will you be all right? I told your maw I'd be staying.'

'I'll be fine. I'm not going anywhere.'

As Hamish put his hand on the door handle, Robbie called out from the lounge, 'What time?'

'Seven o'clock. Be good to see you, Robbie.'

When Mrs Blair arrived back, Robbie had been sleeping, dreaming of football. He was still sitting where Hamish had left him. His skinny legs and Celtic slippers hadn't moved. His legs were sticky, glued to the leather sofa. The television blared out.

'Where's Hamish?' she said, struggling with bags of shopping, her forehead glowing.

'He couldnae stay.'

'What? I told him to stay.'

'There's a football game tonight. The team are playing...'

'And?' Mrs Blair barked back impatiently, unpacking the shopping onto the worktops.

'I just thought I could go.'

'But what's the point, Robbie, if you cannae play?' Then, softening slightly, 'You'll only get upset.'

'Stop being so mean. I wanna go. I'm sick of being around here. I wanna be on a pitch, or near one. Something different.'

Mrs Blair came into the lounge and sat with Robbie. She looked at him, small and listless on the sofa, and put her hand on his.

'Well, okay, we'll go, but don't blame me if it's too much.'

Getting the wheelchair in and out of the car was tricky at first but it quickly became part of their routine. How quickly things do in the face of new challenges. Swivelling himself around so his skinny legs hung from the passenger side of the car, Robbie could see a number of teams warming up on various pitches. He clocked his team straight away. Robbie Blair never missed a trick, and he was getting quicker. In the middle of the pitch he could see the long, lanky frame of Mr McDougal pointing and calling out instructions to the team.

Pushing Robbie across the pitch was harder than expected. Though it was summer, there had been lots of rain and the grass was soft and yielding, and with every push of the chair his wheels sank a little deeper into the turf. Mrs Blair became exasperated, and Robbie, helpless and frustrated, was embarrassed because his friends had begun to see he was there. Eventually, by pulling the wheelchair out of the deepened grooves and pushing forward with a running start, Mrs Blair got Robbie to his destination – the sideline! Hamish ran over to him.

'Robbie! You came!'

'Well, it appears so,' Robbie replied.

Clydebank Primary started well but went 1-0 down early on. They tried to get back into it in the second half but lacked pace up front, especially on the right – Robbie's position. Robbie felt strange. Part of him was into it, with his friends on the pitch, part of the team. But as the light dimmed and the whistle loomed, he drifted away from the team. And when the whistle finally blew, he sat still in his wheelchair watching on, a small silhouette, a footnote to the swirling golden sunset that stretched out behind him.

36

Chapter 9

Back to School

Today was important. It would be the first day back at school. He would be aided by crutches, of course, but – importantly – no wheelchair. He would use his crutches when he got tired and for various tasks: going to lunch, going to the toilet, going to assembly. But, of course, if it had been up to Robbie he wouldn't be using them at all. If it had been up to Robbie, he would have launched them ceremoniously into the River Clyde on his way to school. But he would go with them for a day or two.

Robbie felt his mum was being overly fussy in the Head's office, especially when she kept waving the tatty piece of writing in front of her as she talked. It detailed what Robbie was allowed and, more often, *not* allowed to do. Just leave me now, he thought. It'll be fine. Stop fussing.

'You're made of glass, Robbie, that's why!' she barked at him. 'No more football!' she said, emphasising each word with equal importance. 'I cannae have any more time off work for your broken bones. And you'll end up in a wheelchair. You know what the doctor said.'

'Yeah, yeah,' Robbie muttered. He was always hearing it.

Mrs McClusky politely took Mrs Blair to reception and then came back to take Robbie to class.

'You know she's right, Robbie, and as a school we will continue to support her wishes,' Mrs McClusky told Robbie as they made their way slowly down the corridor – the slightly longer corridor – to his class.

They reached his classroom: P7, the last class before Clydebank High. Morning break was about to start. Loud. How loud they were. Was he this loud too? Sometimes. Before, definitely, and maybe again. But not now, and maybe not for a while. It's hard to be loud on crutches, after all. For a moment, as the pair walked into class, the din continued, but then, as Mr McDougal noticed Robbie and, more importantly, Mrs McClusky, he gave a sharp clap of his hands and a loud command, and then it was pretty much bums on seats, all looking to the Head. And to Robbie. Robbie hadn't been in class, or even school, for six months. He could hear a few whispers. It's Robbie. Robbie's here. Robbie's back.

'P7, may I have your attention, please?' Mrs McClusky said in clipped tones. 'As you can see, Robbie Blair is now back in school. As you can also see, he is still on crutches. We must be extremely careful of Robbie. Treat him as if he was made of glass.'

Really? thought Robbie.

The bell went: time for break. Mini-hysteria broke out. The power of the bell, the whistle.

'Careful,' shouted Mrs McClusky, 'you could cause an accident!' Then, adjusting her glasses and pausing for too long, 'Think of Robbie.'

Robbie had to stay in at breaktime. He was allowed to have a friend to be with him, and could nominate who that might be. A flurry of eager hands went up when Mr McDougal brought this up, as though Robbie was a celebrity. Robbie 'chose' Hamish. Hamish was funny. If he was going to do wordsearches in an empty class, while everyone else was play-ing – well, at least he could be laughing.

Robbie watched through the window. Again. How loud they seemed, even through the double glazing. The power of children all together, playing, not thinking. Timeless. But also strangely out of reach. For now.

Chapter 10

Remembering

Mr McDougal looked at the class.

'So this afternoon we are going to visit an old people's home. We are going to spend the morning thinking of questions that we can ask the elderly people. Remember, old people were just like you once. They had hopes and dreams just like you. They played with toys and grazed their knees, they ran around with a football without a care in the world, and before they knew it they became old and wondered what had happened.'

When the class arrived, they were greeted at the door by a plump lady in her fifties. Mr McDougal signed into the visitors' book and led the children through a succession of rooms until they came to the visitors' lounge. The children snaked sheepishly into the residents' lounge and formed a line underneath the television screen, which was showing a DVD of *Take the High Road* that no one in the room was watching. Robbie and Hamish were directed to a pine dining table at the side of the lounge by the sliding French doors. About four residents were sitting there, mugs of tea in front of them. They were encouraged to colour in some sheets that had been handed out.

A small lady with curly grey hair smiled at Robbie.

'Hello there,' she said. She looked really pleased to see Robbie and his friends.

'Hi,' Robbie said sheepishly.

'Don't be scared. We don't bite,' the lady said.

After a while, Robbie noticed there was a small man in the corner whom no one had noticed. He sat slumped in his armchair.

Robbie went over to him on his crutches. Putting the crutches down, he sat by the man.

'Hi,' Robbie said.

Out of nowhere the slumped, sleeping man opened his eyes and looked at Robbie, startling him.

'Hello to you, young man. You came, then,' replied the man. He was very old – maybe in his nineties.

'Aye,' Robbie replied, a little confused.

'And what's wrong with you, young man?' said the man, looking at Robbie's crutches propped up next to his seat.

'I broke my leg,' Robbie told him.

The man looked at him. 'How did you do that, then?'

'Playing football,' Robbie replied.

'Playing football!' said the man, sitting up a little more. 'Did you get tackled?'

'Aye,' replied Robbie. 'If you can call it that!'

'Well, you know what you should do, then?' the man continued.

'What?' said Robbie staring into the man's deep eyes that had somehow now come completely alive.

'Don't get tackled!'

'Aye, that'd be good,' replied Robbie dreamily.

The man went on. 'Be like Patsy Gallacher! Be quicker. Be the quickest.'

'Patsy who?' Robbie said.

'Patsy Gallacher. The one and only.'

And so it began.

Chapter 11

1925

Patsy Gallacher wakes up early on 11 April 1925. The sound of small children crying and fussing would have been enough to wake anyone bar the heaviest of sleepers, but he is already awake. Big games are nothing new to Patsy. He is a 34-year-old man at the peak of his powers; there is nothing he hasn't seen on the football pitch, no feeling he hasn't felt, no skill he hasn't shown, no trick he hasn't tried. Or so he thought. But today feels different. He knows he isn't getting any younger but, curiously, feels quicker and fitter than ever.
On this day in Renfrew in 1925, as he makes himself a mug of tea, his spindly limbs feel ominously full of life, ready to deliver one more time on the greatest stage of all – Hampden.

As always, the team sheet had been posted up at Celtic Park and all the players had seen this after training on Thursday:

Shevlin; W. McStay and Hilley; Wilson; J. McStay and Macfarlane; Connelly, Gallacher, McGrory, Thomson, and Maclean.

Standard – no surprises there.

The team meets at The Grand Central Hotel in Glasgow city centre. Patsy sits with Jimmy McGrory and talks in short, muscular phrases. The rivet gun hammers into the panel. The strike of the anvil. Patsy moves cutlery and salt and pepper pots to demonstrate his thoughts and visions – well, some of them: the ones he can see. *McGrory nods and smiles wryly.*

What are they saying? What were the words? Flickering images, so far away – voices lost, but now the voices are here. Again.

Willie Maley carefully cuts the mutton on his plate and looks around the room, an emperor surveying his troops. As he casts his eye over the room, he catches Patsy's eye and nods. With a nod the team talk is done, and he pushes his plate neatly to one side.

The players wait for the next tram to arrive, standing outside the imposing Victorian façade of the Grand Hotel. While the kit men deal with the fares, the players are directed to the open-top deck of the No. 22 Glasgow Corporation tram. Sitting towards the back of the tram on the unfurbished wooden seats, Patsy, poker-faced and guttural, arms folded, continues to hammer home ideas for the game. Willie Maley sits at the front of the open-top tram, a wise face soaking in the moments – more of them somehow – as the gleaming orange frontage of the tram cuts through the sea of black and white.

At Hampden, the players disembark the tram and make the short walk to Hampden's East side entrance. The enormous belted wicker baskets containing the kits creak tiredly as they are lifted down from the tram.

75,000 fans wait for the game to start. Another win for Celtic. Routine.

But things don't always go to plan. None of Patsy's gestures and table-top plans seem to have made their way onto the pitch. An inspired Dundee team dominate proceedings and deservedly take the lead after thirty minutes. The 75,000 fans, largely Celtic, are hushed. This was never meant to happen.

Willie Maley stands in the dressing room. His trilby turns to one side as he tweaks his club tie, but he already knows it is immaculately tied. He is thinking.

'You can beat them if you start from the whistle to play the ball and keep playing it all the time. Now then, boys, go on determined to do your very best, and remember the old Celtic spirit.'

The players watch him leave the room.

'It's no' good enough!' Patsy barks, getting to his feet. 'How's this Celtic spirit?'

The words echoing through the players' heads, Celtic are a different force in the second half. Patsy Gallacher, in particular, finally feels the energy in his legs that he felt earlier that morning, and spearheads wave upon wave of dizzying attacks against the Dundee defence. Dundee remain defiant and dogged and hang on despite the shift in momentum. Until. It starts innocuously enough: a loose clearance from Dundee is brought down by a Celtic player and then sent across the pitch to Patsy, a hot rivet at John Brown's thrown across the yard, awaiting its true calling.

All eyes on Patsy. Past the first man in a flicker. Then past the next, a dizzying array of slips, dips, dives, stops, shimmies of magic from another world. At one point, after the fourth man, he puts his boot on the ball and waits. Hampden waits. We all wait. And then, speaking in another language yet to be learned by the lesser mortals on the pitch, he is gone, as if he had never been there at all. On and on towards the goal. The Celtic fans roar him onwards. And then, as quickly as he arrives, it ends. A bruising swipe launches through the air and bulldozes the slender frame of Patsy Gallacher, smashing him to the muddy turf. The Celtic fans groan as one. And it's as if time is paused.

The carrion crows look on from the top of the pavilion grandstand.

The crowd is silent, as if staring back from an old black and white photograph.

'Patsy's down! It's over!' comes a voice from the pitch. The crowd still silent.

And then, as if in slow, Technicolor motion, the magician, the wizard, the mighty atom, ball grasped between his feet, reignited with those words, firing up the embers of his Celtic spirit, lifts himself up. One last time. Staring into the eyes of the statuesque Dundee keeper, Patsy has only one thing in his mind. And it is something he has never thought of before and never will again. Just now. Summoning up all the energies within himself, his skinny legs feel alive and ready to burst. He grabs the wet leather ball between his boots and then springs to life. Up and away, he jumps into the sky like a leaping salmon, a streak of green and white somersaulting over the keeper, ball neatly entwined between his boots. The Celtic fans watch in disbelief as he moves through the air; their breath is held, their hearts are stopped.

And then, as if waking from a dream, they roar as they see Patsy, back on Earth, entangled in the netting of the Dundee goal, the ball still wedged between his boots.

It was like something from another world. It was only the equaliser. But everyone knew. Every Dundee player and every one of the 75,000 fans knew. If ever you could describe an equaliser that seemed like a winning goal, this was that time. Now.

Chapter 12

The Visit

Today had been another momentous and tiring day, another box ticked in Robbie Blair's epic (and not well publicised) comeback trail. He had been allowed to leave his crutches at home. Mrs Blair wasn't convinced at all but caved in as a result of Robbie's relentless, sledgehammer persistence. Robbie did, though, for him, take things carefully. He wasn't going to do anything too stupid – yet. If it was a football game, Robbie came on in the second half for the reserves and had a leisurely amble around the pitch, did some nice things but, importantly, got through it. Of course, this wasn't the best analogy in the world, because Robbie Blair was far from ambling at all, leisurely or otherwise. Yet.

Robbie was now exhausted. But he just couldn't sleep. His head was buzzing. Full of new possibilities that he probably wouldn't be telling his mum about anytime soon. Maybe one day.

So he lay in his bed. Tired. But no sleep. Too tired for sleep. Too much thinking. That in-between state just before sleep, dreaming of dreaming. He would never give up on the dream. He would make it. Robbie repeated the thoughts endlessly. I will make it…

Clank. What was that? thought Robbie. It was a dream. Back at school. Scott had hit the ball at the window; Mr McDougal shouted at him. Sleep. Robbie waited for the ball, poised.

Clank. Again. A sharp noise. On the window. Robbie tensed, and pulled his duvet up nearer his chin.

And then again. Clank. The same sharp knock which defiantly pierced through the hazy twilight of his bedroom, announcing itself. A robin, flying into the window. No, not at this time.

Robbie pushed back his duvet, gingerly lowered his tired, aching leg down to the rough pile of his carpet and then made his way to the window. Slowly pulling the curtains back, he wiped the condensation from the pane. A figure stood in the garden. A man. Skinny-legged, with neat, old-fashioned hair, baggy white shorts and his shirt – the familiar green and white hoops of Celtic. Wait. A drunk, lost his way from the pub. Celtic had played tonight after all. But wasn't the side gate locked?

'What the…?' Robbie thought. The baggy shorts. He'd seen them in books about the history of football. Black and white photos showing barrel-chested football heroes from the olden days.

But this was no book. This was his garden.

Robbie called out. Perhaps it was unwise, but he felt the need somehow.

'Who are you?'

The man looked up. Robbie recognised his face, which seemed to be closer now. Like he was by him, by the window.

'Robbie,' he said.

Chapter 13

Training

One month later

'Sleep tight, love, you've had another busy day,' Mrs Blair whispered through the crack in the door. Robbie, had always liked to have the door slightly ajar to let a little light in. He wouldn't tell his friends that, but he did.

Robbie had had another tiring week. For three weeks now, he hadn't been using crutches at all at school or at home. At first, he felt like he was going to fall over, like his dad used to when he had spent too long at the pub. But bit by bit and day by day, he found the strength and confidence to walk. He was even allowed onto the playground now, though once he'd walked around the edge he would then have to sit on one of the benches and watch his friends play. But his friends were all really good in the main and weren't too rough when he was nearby.

And as he lay in his bed, he started to visualise when he would be able to do more: running, jumping. Wait! Even playing football. Back on the field, as he was before but perhaps even better. Perhaps.

I will play again. I will play again. I will play again.

Robbie felt his hand on the metal latch of the garden gate, which was opening up. The lights of an oncoming car beamed towards him and Robbie looked away, closing the gate behind him. He then slowly peered again onto the main road and, blinking slightly, saw a figure under a street lamp, one of the older ones on Dumbarton Road: in fact, the oldest. He was dressed in baggy shorts and had a green jersey that was almost like a jumper to Robbie but which was tucked into his shorts. He looked at Robbie and seemed to zoom in closer. And, after a while, he smiled.

'Are you ready to start? We've got to get ye strong! Come.'

Robbie had always been told not to talk to strangers, but this was different. And, in any case, he felt like he was still in bed in a way, still home – but also not.

Robbie drifted through the streets. He felt surprisingly light on his feet. He would have to remember this, he thought. Perhaps this was the way he would always have to run: light, like the wind.

Where are we going? he thought. Where were they going? And where was the man? He seemed to have disappeared. But then the football player looked at him, his face so close that Robbie could look deeply into his unblinking eyes.

'We're here,' he said, switching on the lights.

Robbie looked around. It was a large hall, but not a sports hall like he was used to in Clydebank Leisure Centre. There were no five-a-side goals, no brightly coloured tramlines and semicircles. No, here there was a wooden floor made up of tiny, slanted planks that gleamed with a shiny, varnished finish for almost as far as he could see; his face looked back at him in the sheen. Ropes hung down from the ceilings, and the walls were clad with ladders. It was almost as if, Robbie thought, he was on the deck of an ancient ship, ready to set sail. And as he stared into the shiny floor his thoughts and words echoed back and forth.

The figure looked at him, steely, eyes focused, still unblinking. He then pointed at Robbie, and as he did the brow on his angular face furrowed and the lips of his mouth contracted, ready for speech. Robbie could see it all happening as if in slow motion.

And then the figure spoke. 'You need to be strong more than

anything. Strength is the key. From that you can build speed, and then you can add to your skills. And you have skill – of that I'm sure. Listen to what I have to say. With strength you can do anything.' And when he said this, it was if the gymnasium's walls shook – as if Robbie Blair's world shook. Robbie felt it.

'Right. Exercise one. The plank.'

The man lay face down on the gym floor, stretched out straight, propped up by his toes at the back and by his forearms at the front. His fists, which almost met, were clenched with an iron, vice-like intensity. His eyes stared out, his granite face unmoving.

'Go on, try it!' the man called out.

So Robbie got on the floor and placed his body in the same position.

'Straighter! It's nae called a plank for nothing. Be as strong as the girders, Robbie. Be as strong as the ships we built on the Clyde. And no matter how stormy the waters will become, you withstand them, flow with them, but you will always, always be strong and—'

'Afloat?' Robbie added.

The man looked at Robbie and laughed. 'Aye. Afloat. That's gotta help! We cannae have you sinking!'

Chapter 14

Local History

When Robbie Blair woke, he blinked several times and tilted his sleepy head as he waited for the hazy colours of his room to resolve and become clearer. Where had he been? What had he seen? He remembered little parts of it, but was confused. But he also woke with a new-found vigour, a fire in his belly, a spring in his step. All the clichés. But clichés are here for a reason. Because they're good; they do what they say on the tin. And he did have fire in his belly.

Robbie had started to accept that the football dream was over. In the ICT suite at school he had started to google non-contact sports that people who'd broken lots of bones could take part in. One day. Maybe. He also found out he couldn't even go on a trampoline, never mind play football. Google's crap, Robbie thought.

But now something had changed.

He walked to school as normal that morning with Hamish.

'I'm gonna play football again!'

'But you cannae play, Robbie. That's what you said.'

'Aye, but what if I made myself into the strongest, fastest player ever? They'll nae tackle me again and I won't be injured again!'

*

Mr McDougal waited for everyone to sit down in class.

'So, class, in History, till the end of term we are going to be celebrating our history. What we've achieved as Clydebank, as a town, as a community. We're going to be exploring, using what we've got. Or at least what we had.'

Mr McDougal closed his mouth and stared at the back of the room. At somebody. He then began writing on the board, and as he did so he continued, 'So, write in your History books: 'Shipbuilding'. We are going to Clydebank Museum this afternoon.' Robbie smiled. Ever since he'd been back from his latest broken leg, his class seemed to go on endless visits. Bring it on, he thought.

As the children filed into the museum, directed by the attentive Mr McDougal, Robbie caught a glimpse of the Titan Crane gazing into the distance, surveying a wasteland.

Black and white moments of grime, sweat and toil stretched out along the white walls of the museum.

A bearded man from the town also came to talk to the children about shipbuilding. All his family had been shipbuilders, right back to the 1920s – all at John Brown's yard. After break they followed the man down Bruce Street past an old building which used to be the old swimming baths, and went through the fence at the bottom of the road to look at the vast expanse of wasteland where the shipyard actually was. It was hard to imagine now, Robbie thought: just barren scrubland stretching out to the edge of the Clyde.

Chapter 15

The Pool

Robbie was tired. He always was after a day on his feet and, after all, it had only been six months since his latest break, and just over a month since he had put away his crutches. As his eyes closed he thought briefly of playing football again, playing for the school team again, cutting in from the right, twisting and jinking through the defence, crossing in perfectly with his left foot...

A knock-knock at the window. Robbie looked out. It was the figure again: the footballer. Robbie quickly put on his football kit, opened the window and climbed down.

The man gave him the thumbs up and spoke quickly.

'Come on, no time to waste.'

As they ran, the man talked. 'How's the leg?'

'Okay – tired. I've had a busy day. We've been to the shipyard with the school.'

'I know,' said the voice. 'Come,' he continued. 'You havenae played football yet, have you?'

'No, not yet.'

'You will today.'

'Oh, okay,' Robbie replied shyly.

They drifted down past Bruce Street, past the old town hall. They stopped at a door. The man skipped up the steps three at a time; Robbie did his best to follow.

The man pushed through a metal turnstile, the top of which was made of smooth polished wood. It clicked and let them through. Robbie glanced past a wood-panelled kiosk to his right. It was as if there was someone working there – a ledger was open, a pen standing in its holder, a neatly placed file – but there was no one there. They then headed for the light at the end of this small corridor.

'Welcome to our wee pool!' The man was smiling. His eyes twinkled in the light, and the lines that branched out from the corners of his eyes made them look kinder than his voice sometimes sounded. He had on a dark green rugby top, baggy white shorts and old worn-out-looking beach shoes. Behind him lay the rectangular swimming pool, filled with glistening water that sometimes lapped onto the brown-tiled walkway surrounding it. Beyond this walkway a series of white metal rails formed a curtain around the pool, and above them another curtain of rails which signified the floor above. Behind these pretty white criss-cross rails, Robbie could see places for people to change. And above these, a mosaic pattern of blue tiles formed a neat border at the top of the wall and repeated itself all the way around the perimeter of the white pristine hall.

'I havenae got my swimming kit!' Robbie called out to the footballer.

'Dunna worry, laddie, you'll be playing football mostly. But you will get wet.'

'But where?' Robbie was confused.

'In there! Now get in!' the man said, pointing to the pool and clapping his hands. 'Shallow end, Robbie,' he barked again.

Taking his trainers off, Robbie walked over to the shallow end and gingerly dipped his toes into the water.

'Ahh, it's freezing! I'm nae going in there,' Robbie cried out.

Folding his arms, as he liked to do, and turning his square jaw slightly to one side, the man had no time for this.

'Nonsense, don't look so peely-wally. This is a proper pool. Now get in. We havenae got all day!'

Robbie sat on the edge of the pool, drip-fed his feet and skinny legs into the icy water and then slipped in, bracing himself for the inevitable jolt to the system when he was fully immersed. After a few seconds of shuddering, he recovered a little, and the man continued his demonstration.

'Right. To strengthen your legs, you're going to have to train with water, at least for the moment. It will support your wee bones and let you do stuff you wouldnae be able to do on the ground. We can also work on your speed, and some other skills too. If you can be quick in water, you'll be twice as quick as anyone else on a pitch.'

Robbie was asked to do widths of the pool, marching across, and on every third stride he had to raise his knee up. Because it was in threes, each knee thrust used a different knee. Robbie did three sets. His leg felt good in the water – it was the first time he had felt like he was really moving properly again. He felt strong. He felt positive. He had forgotten all about the temperature of the water and was just concentrating on his movement and the words of his teacher.

They then moved through a series of other drills that slightly increased the difficulty – and the strength needed. The man said that when Robbie came swimming in the future, even if it wasn't to this pool, he should incorporate these types of exercises in his training.

He then asked Robbie to move more out of his depth.

'Right, stop there now. We are gonna do a wee bit of running.'

Robbie again looked confused.

'Running! How? And the doctors said running was bad for me.'

'Aye, running on the ground is. It jolts you, like holding a rivet gun at the yard. But I'm taking the floor away, Robbie. Fancy that?'

The man then began to demonstrate by the side of the pool. He began to run slowly on the spot. With slow, hypnotic grace his knee rose up, kicking out in front of him and then retreating back behind in a circular motion before kicking out again. His arms moved in perfect time as his legs performed the running motion – the whole looking like a finely tuned machine. He then demonstrated again with the other leg.

'Now your turn. But do it with these. Remember health and safety, Robbie,' the man said, chuckling and throwing Robbie some ancient-looking floats.

Robbie perched the floats under his skinny arms and, as instructed, moved out so he could no longer feel the tiled floor beneath his feet. The water, reflecting the light from the overhead fittings, projected luminous ripples across the ceiling and walls and, to Robbie's eyes, made the whole hall seem less formed somehow as it swirled around him. And Robbie's teacher seemed to be running at different times and in different parts of the hall, behind him, in front of him, above him.

'Now run, Robbie! Run!' he suddenly announced.

And so, for the first time in months and months, Robbie began to run again. Jerkily at first, but then, as he began to use his legs like pistons, moving forward and back and shifting water like paddles, he began to feel he was starting to float.

'Now, when you're ready! Lose the floats. You can do it, Robbie! Run!'

And, throwing them to one side, Robbie did begin to run effortlessly, marching forth, dancing through the water. He felt alive. Like he'd woken up in the water.

After doing this for a short time, Robbie was guided back to the shallow end.

'How was that, Robbie?' the man asked.

'It was great. If I could train like this, I could be stronger than anyone.'

'Aye, you could. But remember you're a footballer. So, before we finish for the day, catch this!'

Like a sailor throwing a rope to the men on the docks, he threw out what looked like a big leather football attached to a long, weathered rope. Robbie tried to catch the ball, but it was far too heavy and sank to the bottom of the pool. The man positioned himself on the other side of the pool and gave out instructions.

'Robbie, I'm going to pull the medicine ball that's by you towards me, and as it moves pretend you're on a pitch moving forward towards the goal, cutting in from the right, always going forward. But as you do, move your feet over it, step over it, jink with it, dance with it, confuse the defenders. This is good for you. I always went forward, never back!'

And so, for the remaining time in the pool, the man dragged the ball towards him as Robbie moved with it, performing once more, in the watery kingdom of the pool, an array of tricks that he had taught himself to do. And then they were done.

Chapter 16

A Friend

It was Saturday morning, 8am.

A girl was sitting on a bollard, reading a book and looking out across the Clyde. She was wearing jeans and had long, mousey-blond hair, scraped back. She had a pretty face but didn't know it.

Robbie drifted past her, oblivious, weaving a tennis ball through the bollards.

'What you doing?' she called out, glancing up from her book.

Her words stopped him and he looked back.

'You listen sometimes, then?' she carried on.

Robbie shrugged, embarrassed. He didn't really speak to girls very much.

'What you doing?'

'Kicking a ball.'

'I can see. Where to?'

'There!' he said, pointing to the distance. 'And then I come back. That's it.'

'Well, you're real fun, you are,' she mocked. 'I'm Jamie, by the way. Since you're nae gonna ask.'

Robbie came over and sat by her on the towpath.

She noticed his towel sticking out of the rucksack – he'd stuffed it in in a rush. His curly hair was also still wet.

'You been swimming?' she asked brightly.

'Sort of.'

'Sort of?' she smiled. 'Well, you've either been or you haven't – can you nae remember?'

'Well, I have. But not like normal swimming.'

'Ooh, you're hard work, aren't you?' she said, smiling.

Robbie looked awkward for a moment.

'I've been running in the pool,' he explained. Robbie went on to explain what he meant. He talked about his warm-up in the water and the drills he then did. The only thing he didn't mention was who had introduced him to the idea. Not yet anyway. He wasn't sure himself.

Jamie was interested. She'd put her book down and looked at him intently, head slightly to one side. 'Why?'

'Cos I cannae play football. Well, not at the moment anyway. I keep—I mean, I kept breaking bones.'

'Do ya? Did ya? How many?'

'Loads, I guess. The doctor says I'll nae play again. But I stand a better chance of playing again if I get stronger than I was before, stronger than anyone else and faster. But if I train too much on the ground at the moment, my bones might break again.'

'I see. Well, you're a one, aren't you?' she said smiling. 'Well, if you need any help, I'm new round here, but I could give you a hand. Maybe.'

Robbie looked at her. 'Well, sometimes I play football in the pool. I could do with some help then.'

'Okay, I'm in. But only if you help me in return. I wanna get into a team and play football. Could you help me with some of my skills?'

Robbie nodded. 'Aye, that's fine.'

And with that they both walked back home.

Chapter 17

Drills

And so it began. Three times a week Robbie would meet Jamie at 7am at Clydebank Leisure Centre for swimming sessions. She would shout Robbie through various warm-ups and drills and then, for the last part of the session, just as Robbie had done in Bruce Street, she would pull a medicine pool across the width of the pool while Robbie scampered after it, dancing over the ball with various step overs. They got the same strange looks from the early morning lane swimmers of Clydebank, but they didn't care.

'I get it!' Jamie exclaimed after one such session, as Robbie was pulling himself out of the pool. 'So if you get real quick doing these skills under the water, when you're doing them on a pitch you'll be quicker than anyone.'

'Aye, that's the idea,' Robbie said, towelling himself down by the side of the pool and putting his Celtic top on.

Jamie went on, 'And maybe nae get tackled either. That'll be good for your bones, too.'

'Aye,' Robbie said as they wandered out of the pool towards home.

As they walked, Robbie, as ever, dribbled a battered tennis ball, which he then flicked up a couple of times to himself and then passed onto Jamie.

'Robbie?'

'Aye.'

'Where d'ya get the idea for dribbling under the water? It's pretty crazy really when you think about it.'

Robbie stared at her for a while, wondering what he was going to say. But then he just said it. 'I met someone. A footballer. An old footballer.'

'What, like an old man?'

'No. Not an old man. An old footballer.'

'Now you are confusing me, Robbie. How d'ya do that, then?'

'I don't know, Jamie. I don't know. I went to bed and sort of ended up somewhere else.'

'Ah, like a dream, then!' said Jamie, feeling she was finally getting somewhere.

Robbie rubbed his fingers through his loose, curly hair, looked into the distance and then fixed his eyes on Jamie once more. 'Aye, Jamie, maybe like a dream. But I think I left the room. I think I left the house.' Robbie's voice trailed off.

'Like sleepwalking?'

Robbie thought for a moment. No, not walking. It was never walking. Too quick for that. Whatever it was.

'Kinda,' Robbie answered.

'You know what?' he said, looking straight ahead into the distance again and changing the subject. 'I'm gonna start running.'

'Are you sure you're ready?'

'Aye, I think so. I think I'm ready for solid ground again! But I'm gonna treat it like water. But now,' Robbie said, pointing to the John Brown pitches, 'your turn!'

Chapter 18

Night Flight

The moon hung full and white in the sky above. Under its gaze, Robbie breezed down the street. There, waiting under the golden haze of the street lamp, stood the man. He had his back to him but then, as Robbie approached, he turned. He gave a craggy smile and then a command to start running. They ran into the night, which stretched out in front of Robbie like an endless road heading for a singular illuminating point on the horizon. But, as well as seeming distant, the point they headed for, wherever that was, seemed both there and here to Robbie. There and here.

There didn't appear to be many cars on the road, Robbie thought – and how straight the road seemed! Perhaps everything seems straight and in one direction when you are in the moment.

After a while, the man gave the signal to slow down. Five, four, three, two, one. Robbie didn't think this was necessary – he could see if someone was slowing down, walking or stopping. But he always gave in nonetheless – the man was the coach, after all. The run was important, he said, and it should form the bedrock of Robbie's fitness sessions. He also told Robbie to speed up between every other lamp post and to walk between the intervening ones. This struck a chord with Robbie. I will always do this, he thought.

'The best footballers,' the man said, 'can react and think well when under pressure and when tired. Normally, when players are tired, things go – speed, technique and then thinking. So it is important to feel tired before we start, so we can work on your endurance.'

He looked at Robbie hard and still, as he always did when he had a point to make. When he had a point to make, people listened.

Turning off Cathcart Road, they entered what seemed like a park. They walked up a slight incline, skipping up some wooden steps through a scattering of young trees. At the top of the bank, they headed down.

'Watch your step,' said the man, leading the way. Robbie looked down as he walked carefully over the series of small stone steps, avoiding the wild tangle of branches and undergrowth that crept over them like a threadbare carpet.

'Mind that!'

Too late. Clunk. Robbie felt something hard and metallic knock his shoulder. He reached for it, and felt how it came straight and true out of the concrete steps and then flat for a while before going back into the steps. It had been painted once, but the paint and rust sprinkled into his hand as he brushed along it.

'What even is this?' Robbie asked, pointing at the metal bar. 'And what are these steps leading to? What is this place?'

'Cathkin Park!' came the voice. 'Come on. Onto the pitch!'

'What pitch?' asked Robbie, following him down the steps.

The man vaulted the remaining steps, which were more visible now under the full moon, skipped onto some kind of gravelly track and then, when he reached the grass a few yards later, jumped around excitedly.

'This pitch!' he shouted, gesturing all around him. His voice seemed to echo back and forth in Robbie's mind.

As Robbie looked, it was as if someone had switched on the lights. Clear and crisp under the spotlight of the moon lay a beautiful football pitch. It was as though they were in a magical room. It seemed to be both from another world and also strangely familiar. A wonderfully flat carpet of green grass lay in the centre. Around the pitch, a curtain of trees rose up, a jagged silhouette that gave way to the deep midnight blue of the sky.

'Right, Robbie. We haven't got much time left,' he said, holding the ball in front of him.

'But we've only just got here. And we haven't practised anything yet.'

'I mean *we* haven't got much time left. I cannae help ye forever, can I?'

He paused. And when he paused, it was as if time itself stood still.

He went on, 'So. We've done strength, we've done speed. Is there anyone as strong as you at school?'

Robbie shook his head.

'Is there anyone as fast as you?'

'Not now,' Robbie said.

'Aye, and is there anyone as small as you?' the man chuckled. 'So now I want us to look at dribbling. Come on! Get the ball off me.'

He glided and danced around the pitch, with the ball seemingly glued to his boot. With the inside, then the outside of his foot, dropping his shoulder, dragging the ball, it was a flurry of movement and magic that seemed too quick for the eye, thought up and executed on the spot. As if he wasn't thinking at all. As if he existed only in the moment. And he did, of course. It all did.

Two hours were spent, though it felt like thirty seconds. Jinks, dinks, step overs, step unders and steps that didn't have a name, couldn't be described, were all looked at, broken down to isolated movements and then built back up to the desired pace. Whatever that was.

'Too slow! I can see what you are doing. I can follow the movement of your foot. Too slow. Again, too slow. You need to move like the wind. No pressure. But be like the wind. A ghost. You're seen and then you're gone.'

'Is that like you, mister?' asked Robbie, the ball at his feet.

'Just be quicker. Be quicker. Practice over.'

When Robbie reached his side gate, he paused to look back for the footballer, but he had gone, melted into the night. As Robbie fastened the latch on the gate, the distant, familiar hum of the milk float could be heard drifting through the dawn light towards him.

Robbie climbed into his bed and lay there. Be quicker, he thought.

Chapter 19

The Night

It started like a whisper but then engulfed him, swept him up in the darkness.

> 'Willie Maley was his name
> He brought some great names to the game
> When he was the boss at Celtic Park
> He taught them how to play football
> He made the greatest of them all
> Gallacher and Quinn have left their mark.
>
> [Chorus:]
> And they gave us James McGrory and Paul McStay
> They gave us Johnstone, Tully, Murdoch, Auld and Hay
> And most of the football greats
> Have passed through Parkhead's gates
> For to play football the Glasgow Celtic way.'

Mr McDougal wavered a while on the steps of the Working Men's Club. Celtic had done their job in the Europa League – not quite on the path to the glory years of 1967, but on their way. He'd had a busy week at school. The new Head had started and was very paperwork-orientated, which was not Mr McDougal's strength. He was the kind of teacher who looked organised but wasn't really.

Robbie drifted past him. As if the people he was talking to had been muted by a supreme being, Robbie floated past in the hazy night. The beer slowed Mr McDougal's brain, but his eyes were tuned in.

'Robbie! It's me – Mr McDougal!'

Robbie's unmistakable green and blue eyes looked at Mr McDougal. They looked through him.

The figure carried on running.

Chapter 20

The Dream

The plus side of going to the Royal Hospital for Children, Glasgow for an appointment to see Dr Klaus Hergler, world expert on bone density in children, was that Robbie had a day off school. And missed Maths. This was becoming a habit, Robbie thought.

'Robbbbbbieeee! Will you get a move on!' bellowed his mum from downstairs.

Robbie still lay in bed. Motionless. He knew what the doctor was going to say. He'd said it all after his second break eighteen months before. Unusual to break a femur…blah blah blah…strongest bone in the body…blah blah blah…almost impossible to break…apparently not!… blah blah blah. No contact sport…blaaahhhh, blaaahhhh…blaaahhh! What was the point in going? Ooh, Robbie shouldn't have been playing football again and, lo and behold, he's broken his femur again. Yes, the hardest bone to break. He knew what he was going to say, all right. He could say it for him.

'Robbbbbbbbbbbie! We're gonna miss the train!'

The children's hospital was a scary-looking building, especially for children. Huge sandstone walls with pointed towers and arches. It looked like something out of a scary film set in Victorian times. The type where a small angelic child in a cloth cap suddenly appears out of nowhere, standing by a fountain, and then just as suddenly disappears. They did their best inside. Murals showing princesses and Winnie the Pooh and gingerbread cottages could sugar-coat the whole experience but, for Robbie, the damage had already been done.

But that was just one reason. The main reason that he hated the children's hospital was nothing to do with sandstone or arches or scary-looking windows. It was because, to Robbie, hospital meant the end of the dream – his footballing dream. And that could really put you off a place far more than architecture ever could.

'The doctor will see you now,' said the fussy receptionist. Robbie's mum jumped up and led the way. Robbie, sullen, trudged behind.

It was a small room. A bed. Some chairs. A bookshelf with books and folders about bones and kids and kids' bones. A big kid-friendly poster of a human skeleton stared down at Robbie from the cold stone wall. Robbie's eyes were drawn to the femur – the unbreakable thigh bone – the king of the bones.

'Ah, Robbie. And mum. How are you both?' His German accent was strong and clinical-sounding. 'Robbie has now broken major bones five times.'

I know, Robbie thought. I was there.

'Including,' he went on, 'his femur three times.'

Aye, and was still there for those, too.

'Now, the femur is the strongest bone in the body.'

Please don't, Robbie thought.

'It is almost impossible to break,' the doctor continued, waving his glasses.

'Well, apparently not,' said Robbie.

'Sssh, Robbie,' snapped Mrs Blair.

'It is fine, Mrs Blair. The boy is sad.'

We know all this, thought Robbie. Why are you telling me stuff I already know?

'We've looked at the bone density results and...'

What was he going to say? What about the bone density scan? Robbie thought, yearning to know, scared to find out.

'So, Robbie,' the doctor continued, 'as I may have said before, when I say "bone density", think of it like this. A cake has a low density and can be broken up easily. A biscuit has a high density and so is stronger and won't easily fall apart.'

What would he say next? Robbie sat, pouring his mind into Dr Hergler's brain. What would he say?

'And we've decided they fall into the category that we tend to call perfectly normal, so, as far as we can see, Robbie has just been unlucky with his multiple fractures, and so we can see no actual reason why he shouldn't return immediately to playing competitive football.' Game on!

But that was not what he was going to say; and indeed, that was not what he said.

'Yes, I'm afraid the scans show, as I feared – as *we* feared – that Robbie's bone density is very low, and falls into one of the lowest categories,' he said, pointing to a very low point on the bone density graph.

This was a low point, Robbie thought.

There was a lower part to the graph that Robbie was higher than. That, presumably, was for the kids made of cake. Robbie thought for a second, Great. I'm stronger than cake, weaker than biscuit – wait: I'm a Jaffa cake!

'So what happens now, Doctor?' asked Robbie's mum. Robbie said nothing.

'Well. The good news is that we can offer Robbie some medical treatment to help him with his bone density.'

That did get Robbie's attention. Treatment. He hadn't anticipated this. Treatment! This wasn't in the script that he had gone over and over and over as he lay awake in his bedroom, too fed up to sleep. Or to dream.

'Yes, Robbie will come back here twice a year and will receive calcium-boosting medicine via a drip. Each procedure will last about forty-five minutes and…'

Forty-five minutes, Robbie thought – that's the first half…

'What will that do? Does that mean I'll play football again?'

'No, sadly not, Robbie. Based on all the data I have before me and based on your multiple fractures, I must urge you that, even with treatment, you really must never play contact sport again. It is too risky. Far too risky. If you were mine, you would never play football again.'

'Don't worry, Doctor, his football days are done. Aren't they, Robbie?' said his mum annoyingly. 'I said, aren't they, Robbie?'

Robbie said nothing. His eyes filled up and he thought if he moved an inch the tears would spill over and run down his face. A never-ending flow.

'I'm sorry, Robbie. But that's where we are.'

But Robbie knew where he was. He didn't need telling.

Chapter 21

The Goal

'Right, class,' Mr McDougal said, facing his Primary 7s. 'Tests out of the way. For the rest of the week you can carry on working on your projects for the end-of-year assembly.'

Great, Robbie thought, another day to research the football players Fred had talked to him about during his visits to the home; another day to lose himself in the wet and windy games of Scottish football's yesteryears.

'It always seemed wet and windy then,' Robbie mused. 'Perhaps that's what the past does? Makes it wetter and windier.'

'Aw, you kidding me?' replied Hamish. 'You've lived in Clydebank your entire life! It's always wet and windy now – that's why we have so many 4G pitches in Scotland!'

Robbie sat at a computer in the corner of the ICT suite. He logged on, googled a match on the Celtic Wiki from a year he hadn't yet been to and…

And then Robbie was away, back to…1921.

Match Report, The Scotsman, 20 September 1921
17,000 fans eagerly awaited the clash of top of the table Celtic against an injury-stricken Hibernian. The Hibs team had been plagued by a spate of

misfortunes in recent games and had to reshuffle massively for this important encounter.

> *The experiment was made of playing Paterson at centre forward. Shaw was at centre-half, and the vacancy in the middle line was filled by the inclusion of Strang. Templeton played for McGinnigle, who was still injured, and Walker was at outside-left. The first half was evenly contested – honours even. At the start of the second half the Hibs were mostly aggressive, but they did not take their chances, though Ritchie struck the crossbar when Celtic goalkeeper Shaw was out of his goal, and Paterson had more than one good attempt to find the net, one in particular when he caught the ball in the air and came near scoring with a hit-or-a-miss effort. It was to Paterson that the first goal fell, and a nice hook of his it was that beat Shaw.*

Willie Maley watches from the stand, unmoved. The rain is stronger now and makes ashen puddles on the terraced steps. Maley's face moves steadily, following the ball around the sodden pitch below.

'What the hell?' A short, squat man shouts towards the pitch. 'Give it to Patsy! It's nae difficult, boys!'

McGrory taps the ball to the slender figure of Patsy Gallacher. He has pulled his shirt out, which now hangs down over his white mud-splattered shorts. Patsy drags the ball back under his white-laced boot and takes in the scene before him. It's as if he pauses the game. And as he is pelted from the heavens by Scottish rain, he is drenched in the possibilities that lie ahead – mapped out, ready to perform. First tackle comes in. Patsy swiftly jumps over his foot and pushes the ball on. Another shimmy and gone. Another boot sliding through the mud, another hop. He is simply too quick. And onward he goes, three challenges and counting, now entering the barren no man's land between the centre circle and the eighteen-yard box.

'That's more like it! Go on yoursel'!' hollers the squat man from the stands. In the rain, Maley looks on.

A fourth challenge comes and goes and then five, six and seven are *all left floundering bewildered in the mud as Patsy dances on towards the eighteen-yard box. Cutting in from the right, Patsy drops his shoulder and swiftly darts past another like a wild deer. Eight. Nine arrives, panic in his eyes. Patsy casually puts his foot on the ball and his hands on his shorts. He looks at the crowd, who roar him on. Nutmegging the ninth, he has one defender left to beat before the goalkeeper. The full back has his legs closed, knees almost touching, knowing what to expect. Patsy, as if back at John Brown's, knows what to do. Hitting the ball at the 'metal girders' standing in front of him, he races on to the ball, catching it with the outside of his foot. Only Billy Harper to beat.*

Harper is a class keeper who plays for Scotland. But he is Patsy's eleventh man; he has beaten an entire team. He skips effortlessly over Harper's dive and scores with a gentle tap. Just a gentle tap. After dribbling past an entire team. A gentle tap. The Celtic fans roar. The squat man hollers. Maley smiles.

'Robbie!' shouted Callum as he peered over his shoulder to see what he was looking at on the computer. 'Why you even reading this?' Callum went on. 'Celtic losing to Hibs 2-1! You're obsessed!'

Chapter 22

1916

Robbie suddenly decided, after running home from school, that he was going to run past his house and on to the care home to see Fred.

As Robbie made his way to the lounge, the familiar, nondescript teatime smell wafted through the snaking corridor. The carer, a young girl in her early twenties, gently touched Fred's hand, which was resting on the faded fabric of the armchair that he sat in.

'Robbie's here, Fred, isn't that nice?'

As she did this, Robbie suddenly noticed that Fred had only one leg. He didn't know why he hadn't noticed before, but he hadn't. His left leg was missing.

The girl winked at Robbie and left them.

'So, Robbie,' he said, opening his eyes. 'I've been waiting for you. Now, where were we?'

A biting gusty wind swirls around Celtic Park, playing havoc with the passes of both sides. All too often a well-intentioned pass goes astray, ballooning into the crowd like a rock being tossed around by a wild, tempestuous sea.

Celtic are playing Rangers. Another derby. The clock on the old grandstand says 4:33pm. From the sound of the crowd, it appears as if it is a draw at the moment. Celtic are being urged on by most of the 103,000 capped spectators. A draw does look likely as the final whistle looms.

But some still believe.

A small, skinny man in a hooped shirt is given the ball. A quick drag back, a ghostly feint and he's gone, cutting through the Rangers defence. His name is Patsy Gallacher. It is 1916.

Just the goalkeeper stands between him and another glorious moment in his already impressive career. He stops; he looks the Rangers keeper in the eye. The keeper is confused, totally unaware of which way the maverick inside right will go. Patsy decides to go right and, neatly hopping the outstretched, grasping advances of the beaten goalkeeper, is through. But just at this moment, steaming in like a train, a burly, faceless figure slides in from behind. From the shadows. Out of nowhere.

Like a rivet being hammered into a sheet of metal, Gallacher is smashed into the muddy quagmire of the six-yard box by the mid-air, brutal two-footed challenge. Gallacher tries to move his left leg but the shooting pain, already present, becomes unbearable.

'I cannae move it!' he cries out to Jimmy Quinn, the big, broad-shouldered Celtic striker, who looks down at Patsy like a seasoned coal miner at the scene of an explosion.

Quinn tries to help Gallacher to his feet, but Gallacher cannot put any weight on the stricken leg and he lies back down on the muddy turf.

'It's broken, Quinny! It's over!'

Quinn gestures to the stand and two men run onto the pitch with a stretcher. Gallacher is carefully moved onto the stretcher so as not to further damage his shattered leg, and they make their way to the side of the pitch. In a world where, in distant lands, pleasant pastures are being transformed into hellish wastelands, Gallacher is stretchered off – a wounded soldier leaving the battlefield.

As he makes his sorry way to the touchline, the Rangers defender, the very same assassin who had brought him down, appears at his side, staring down, glowering over him.

'I'm awful sorry, Patsy, about the leg,' he says, grinning.

In an instant, Gallacher flies at him from his stretcher with a flying *kick from his right leg. His boot connects perfectly with the defender, straight between the legs. The defender collapses in a pathetic, crumpled heap.*

'Aye, but I've still got this one!' Gallacher says, staring down at the hapless defender.

Chapter 23

Found Out!

10:35am Saturday.

There was a knock at the door. 'Robbie! Can you nae get that?'

'Fine,' Robbie said, switching off his PlayStation game and trudging downstairs.

He opened the door as far as the chain would allow and peered through the small gap. He stared through and out, up to the face of a man looking down at him. The man's face looked big, amplified and distorted, like Robbie was looking into a back of a spoon. It was Mr McDougal.

'Is your maw in?'

'Aye.'

'Can I see her?'

'Maybe,' said Robbie unhelpfully.

'Like, now.'

Robbie slipped the chain and let his teacher in.

'Mr McDougal!'

Robbie's mum suddenly went from shouting to using a warmer, gentler tone. She propped up cushions and picked up football magazines and bowls of cereal.

Mr McDougal sat down. He was in his late forties. He was tall and slim, and looked organised in a friendly way. He had dark hair that was curly but, because it was cut short and neat, it couldn't remember how curly it really was. Robbie's mum liked him. Robbie could tell.

'How are you, Robbie?' asked Mr McDougal.

'I'm good,' replied Robbie, as all children do. Robbie's mum smiled with that smile that is pretending to smile and convinces no one at all.

'We are worried about you, Robbie.'

Robbie shrugged without actually shrugging.

'What you been doing, Robbie?' Robbie's mum cried out. 'Not playing football again? Please God, no. D'you wanna end up in a wheelchair? Cos that's what'll happen!'

'I've not been playing football, I swear!' Robbie shouted back.

The teacher went on, 'Mrs Blair. How can I put this?' Mr McDougal bent his head forward and stroked his chin. 'Robbie has been seen on several occasions running down Dumbarton Road in the middle of the night to God knows where.'

Mrs Blair rose up from the sofa, aghast. 'What do you mean? Running in the middle of the night? Who with?'

'That's the thing, Mrs Blair. According to Kevin McGonagall, who was on his way back from the post office, he was running by himself. Alone.'

Robbie sat there on the sofa, taking it all in. Confused.

'Mrs Blair, I have a duty at the school to safeguard the welfare of all the students. I'm sure you are a lovely mother to Robbie, and I won't report this to anyone at the moment, but—'

'What the hell, Robbie?' interrupted Mrs Blair. 'Do you wanna get taken into care?'

'What?'

'If it looks like I cannae look after you properly, you'll end up in a care home. Is that what you want?'

'No.'

'What are you doing running around Clydebank in the middle of the night? Are you mad? Do you need to go and see somebody again?'

And Robbie thought to himself: maybe he was mad.

Chapter 24

Shipbuilding

As usual, the man stood under the street lamp, but tonight the rays from the old lamp splashed light onto different clothes. He wasn't dressed in football kit at all. Strange, Robbie thought.

'We're going to do things differently today,' he announced, pointing his fingers. 'We cannae have you in any more trouble, can we?' he continued as they made their way down past the town hall.

Wasn't it tonight, not today? Robbie thought. Somehow it didn't matter, but he wasn't sure why.

They walked down Dumbarton Road past the town hall. Same as ever.

'What we gonna be looking at today?' Robbie asked. 'I've been running like you said. Getting up before school and running past the Titan. And I've been stopping and then flying off again like you said.'

The footballer looked at him. His eyes lit up the darkness. 'You still need to be quicker and stronger! Than anyone.' Turning round and looking at Robbie, boring into his eyes. 'And you need to use what you've got!'

'You mean use what I am?'

'I mean use what's around you! Use what's around you!' the man said. The voice was still there in the night air, but the face had gone.

'Around you,' it said again.

Robbie looked around, down the street, to his left, to his right and back. Where had it come from? Nothing.

Then the voice. Again.

'Now. Close your eyes,' the voice said. 'Where did you go?' he called out to Robbie.

Robbie opened his eyes. He was still here. Still by the town hall clock. The lamp. The road. It was the same width, but the road – the road was uneven. He tripped.

'Mind yourself. You're always losing your feet,' the man said kindly.

How did he know what I did? Robbie thought.

It was lighter. It seemed like day. Maybe early morning. How long had they been talking? Robbie wondered. The uneven ground was caused by the cobbled surface that had somehow replaced the modern tarmac that Robbie was used to. Robbie looked down at the uneven stones that now formed the foundation of his reality. Was this real?

'Here! Have your ball back!' he called out, throwing his tennis ball at Robbie. 'Keep control of it now,' he barked. 'On yer toes. Like a goat.'

And then they came. From a distance. At first one or two and then more, gathering in number with every passing moment. As they got closer, Robbie could see what they were wearing. Man after man, all wearing caps, most with moustaches. All dressed the same, all looking ahead. When the mob of men reached him, their big, cumbersome boots echoing through the cobbled street, their eyes looked right through Robbie as if he wasn't there.

Robbie turned round as they streamed past him, around him, through him.

'Where are we?' Robbie asked, confused.

He looked at him and looked at the men, who were turning right and drifting through the wrought-iron gates of John Brown's Shipyard.

'You're here. Always here.'

'What the hell?' Robbie said. 'Where are they going?'

'Come,' beckoned the man, whisking the tennis ball away from Robbie's feet. 'Welcome to John Brown's Shipyard.'

Robbie had heard of John Brown's Shipyard. They had studied it for a local history project led by Mr McDougal. To be honest, to a degree, everyone knew about shipbuilding in Clydebank. It was what had made Clydebank.

The shipyard unravelled beautifully before Robbie in the clear light – an ever-changing flow of cranes and crates, men and machines, circling and dwarfing him from the ground to the sky; everything, everywhere at once and together. As Robbie followed him further into the yard, it ebbed and flowed in front of him like a tide, as though someone was directing a film, moving scenery in and out, the story moving on and on and back and forth. How busy everywhere was. Was this really Clydebank? His home. The wasteland.

And so began their tour of the yard. First, they walked into a big building, where groups of men had long sheets of metal spread out on the floor. At regular intervals, they made marks on the sheets with a special tool, kneeling down but moving briskly across the metal with neat efficiency, rolled-up cigarettes perched in the corner of their mouths.

'So they know where to put the rivets,' the man said, pointing.

'What's a rivet?' Robbie asked.

'What's a rivet? Kids, eh?' the man answered back, joking with the capped worker, who muttered something and carried on marking out. 'They hold the ships together, so they do! Like the rivets in your leg, Robbie! Here!' he shouted as he reached into a bucket and threw a small metal bar towards Robbie. Robbie caught it and examined it in his cupped hand. It was about eight centimetres long and three centimetres wide, and one end had a rounded, moon-shaped cap. Robbie put it into the pocket of his shorts and looked for the footballer, who had already skipped on to the next part of the yard.

Moving towards the water, huge metal frames rose from the ground on either side of the slip, interlocking with other frames, creating a giant, criss-crossing mesh of girders. And there, as if suspended within this metal cage, stood the enormous hull of the ship, only partly built but impressive nonetheless, like an iron whale, mouth gaping, cut adrift from the sea.

'Look, Robbie. Rivets!'

A gloved man held metal tongs in a small furnace, turning away as the embers from the flames swirled into his eyes and landed on his sweaty exposed forearm. He pulled the tongs from the fire, placed the white-hot rivet between his gloves and threw it to the next man along, who caught it in his gloves, then it was thrown to the next and then the next, now higher towards the top of the scaffold, a seamless chain; the rivet was like a pebble skimming through the air until it reached its destination. The man then put the now red-hot rivet in a hole in the panel using his metal tongs and then hammered it in with a riveting gun. Seconds after the rivet had emerged newly born from the fiery furnace, it had moved thirty yards to its final destination and was now fixed in place, cooling and tightening the sides of the ship.

'It's amazing!' Robbie said, transfixed. 'It's like a game.'

Suddenly the deafening sound of the siren – or the finishing whistle – blared out, and everyone stopped their work. It was half-time.

'Hey, Patsy!' called a man, kicking a football to him. 'You joining us?'

'Na, I'm good,' the man said, producing a ball from nowhere and leading Robbie away from the swarm of men to a quieter part of the yard.

'Here! This is where I practise!'

They stood in an open space in the yard, surrounded by rolls of metal and girders that were awaiting the next stage of their journey. The process.

He placed some metal buckets at different intervals for dribbling. He then propped up two metal girders next to each other before finally placing two wooden boxes about ten yards apart. He then produced a pair of light training shoes from the pocket of his trousers and changed out of the clumpy work boots he had been wearing.

'Right! Watch!'

He weaved in and out of the buckets with skilful guile, no slower with the ball than if he had been running alone. At one with the ball. Robbie watched in awe as he reached the girders. He put his foot on the ball and looked at Robbie, eye to eye. He then smashed the ball purposefully at the left girder and pounced immediately on the ricochet, which had been propelled forward, and then eased the ball between the two wooden boxes.

'See!' the man barked. 'That's all for today. Let's get on now, laddie.'

Robbie looked at his teacher.

'Are you Patsy Gallacher?'

The man looked at Robbie. Robbie looked at the man.

'Aye,' he replied. 'Maybe.'

Chapter 25

The Sparrow

It was 6am. The birds woke Robbie. He never used to listen to the birds, but now he did. Patsy was right. If he was ever going to recover and make a comeback… Comeback. If he was ever to do that, he would have to practise what Patsy was telling him. Really practise. And use what he had.

Up. And out. And now.

Everything was still and quiet. He gently opened the front door and peered out cautiously, looking up either end of the road. Was it safe? Safe enough.

'Morning, Robbie,' the milkman called out as he quietly hummed past. He was okay, he was fine. Not like the others.

No other cars. Check. No people. Pretty much. Run.

Robbie turned off Dumbarton Road and cut down a side road that led to the Titan. Clambering the bars of the metal gate, he sat, poised. The sky was still waking up. Strips of grey blending into pinks, moving into bright light. He looked at the Titan, etched onto the canvas in black ink. Big. Proud. Surveying all. Still. Here.

A sparrow landed on the steel frame next to Robbie. The sparrow looked at Robbie. Robbie jumped and landed with a thud. He turned around to see the sparrow, which had flown away.

Robbie ran over the abandoned scrubland to the Titan. As he ran, he planned his routine. What was he here to do? What would be achieved? He was set. Finding a patch of ground that was roughly the length of the penalty area, he threw his jumper down and then paced about eighteen yards to the tumbledown remains of an old brick wall – or was it a forge?

Having finished his training, he sat on the old brick remains. Suddenly grabbed by an urge, he climbed up and perched on top of it. The sparrow flew back and stood by him, peering up, peering down. Both curious, both looking. Jump! Easy feet. Easy knees. Robbie jumped and landed in the wasteland without a sound. Nothing. He turned. The sparrow looked.

Chapter 26

Dreams

Robbie Blair was running on the towpath past the Titan. Jamie sat watching him.

'Hi,' said Jamie.

Robbie slowed down and looked at her. 'You all right?'

'Robbie, I've been thinking about what you told me. About your dreams. With the footballer. My dad is a professor at Glasgow University and he said…'

Robbie looked away into the distance.

'Well,' she said, folding her arms. 'Do you want me to tell you what my dad said?'

Robbie looked at her, not knowing what to say. He felt blank. He was confused but didn't know what to say to her.

'He said that people have dreams when they are in a really deep sleep, after they have been asleep for quite a while – that's what they call REM sleep. At that point, people dream but they can't move. Their brain won't let them move – it would be too dangerous. So my dad doesn't think you would be able to dream and run around at the same time. Well, it's really unusual, anyway.'

Robbie looked at her and felt irritated in a way. 'I can't help what

I saw or felt. I met someone and I was running around town. I'm not making this up! It is just what it is. Just let me practise.'

Jamie looked hurt. 'Can I come too?'

'Aye, all right.'

Robbie was silent on the way to the football pitch. He had been confused before, but now he was even more confused.

'I'm not saying you were making it up, Robbie. He's a scientist. He deals with facts and figures all the time. That's his life.'

Chapter 27

Mr McNeil

The next day, on the way to school, Hamish caught up with Robbie and called to him.

'Hey, Robbie!'

'Is training on next week?' Robbie asked, not blinking.

'Aye,' Hamish said, as the boys walked into school.

Mr McDougal walked into class with a man who looked to Robbie like he was about twenty, but he was probably older. When all the children had sat down and stopped fussing, Mr McDougal started talking.

'So, children, this is Mr Ryan McNeil. Mr McNeil will be teaching PE at the school from now on. We are very lucky to have Mr McNeil at the school, because he has represented Scotland in the Commonwealth Games at both swimming and gymnastics.'

Mr McNeil, slim but clearly muscular, stood and looked a little embarrassed as the accolades were heaped upon him.

Hamish whispered to Robbie, 'Pity he's not a footballer, though.'

'Aye, maybe, but he's represented Scotland. And do you realise how strong you have to be to be a gymnast?' Robbie replied, still looking at Mr McNeil.

Later on, in PE, Mr McNeil spoke to the children in the hall. 'So, hello, everyone.'

'Good morning, Mr McNeil,' the children replied robotically.

'So for the rest of the autumn term we will be looking at gymnastics. I know y'all have done gymnastics before but maybe I'll show you something more. Something else.'

Robbie sat listening, legs stretched out on the polished, planked floor. He couldn't sit cross-legged like the other kids. He hadn't been told not to, but a year after his last break he found it too difficult. Not painful, just resistant, as if his bones had a mind of their own, as if they were telling him. No. Not yet. He just knew.

The hall was laid out with a trail of mats which wound their way around the room on a meandering journey, eventually ending near the entrance. At the end of the trail lay a springboard and then two deep blue mats.

Mr McNeil peeped his whistle. The children all looked at him attentively.

'So, the forward roll! I'm guessing you've all done a forward roll before. But I don't know that. Show me. Impress me.'

Mr McNeil had his arms folded, waiting to be impressed, as he had said.

'To the beginning, anyway. Stand. Kneel. Then put your hands in front, spread out. But don't just put them out. They should be holding you – feel your body through your hands.'

As he was demonstrating this, some of the children looked around and fidgeted, glancing at the dinner ladies turning up for work and walking up the corridor to the school kitchen.

But Robbie was transfixed.

Mr McNeil went on, 'Next you need to rock forward, let yourself down and land on the top of your back, missing your head. Don't land on your head. And keep your legs tucked in – don't throw them out. Nice and neat. Nice and quiet. Easy.'

The children lined up in three groups at different points around the hall, awaiting their turn.

Hamish whispered to Robbie. 'You shouldnae be doing this, Robbie, I'm guessing.'

Robbie ignored him, concentrating, looking at his hands.

The children performed their rolls with varying degrees of success. Some of the boys landed on their heads to comic effect. Some of the girls who attended out-of-school gym classes were perfect in their delivery, even jumping up after the roll. Perfect. Neat. No sound. Then came Robbie's turn.

He was nervous, but also not nervous, if that were possible.

He bent forward and stretched out his hands on the floor and waited till it felt right. Then he pushed himself forward, hands spread out, absorbing, feet tucked in, spinning around and landing, lightly, like the bird by the Titan. But, instead of landing on his bottom, Robbie found himself on his feet. Perched, ready for the next.

'Very good. Nice,' Mr McNeil said. 'You're strong!'

Just then, Mr McDougal burst through the double door to the hall.

'I'm sorry, Mr McNeil, but can I have a quick word?'

'Of course,' said Mr McNeil, walking towards the door to the hall. Robbie watched Mr McDougal whisper to Mr McNeil. He watched really intently.

'Robbie Blair, can I have a wee word, please?' Mr McDougal called.

'Aye,' Robbie said, walking over to them.

'I've just been telling Mr McNeil that you shouldn't be doing gymnastics. My mistake, Robbie. Your maw had told us.'

Robbie looked at Mr McDougal and Mr McNeil. 'Just let me know when I'm allowed to do something.'

'That's just the way it is, Robbie,' said Mr McDougal, looking at him for a moment before walking off.

As Mr McNeil dismissed the class for lunch, he patted Robbie on the back. 'That was good, Robbie. Very good.'

Chapter 28

Psychologist Again

On Friday, after Maths, Mr McDougal walked up to Robbie and asked him if he would follow him to the office.

As they walked down the corridor Mr McDougal looked at Robbie. 'It's all right, you've done nothing wrong.'

Robbie nodded but was suspicious.

Robbie walked into Mrs McClusky's office and, to his surprise, saw his mum and the psychologist man. Again.

'Hello, Robbie. Come and sit down by your mum. Your mum's been telling me you're doing well, Robbie.'

'Aye.'

The psychologist looked over his spectacles at Mrs Blair. 'So, how's he been generally?'

'Much better, Doctor. He seems more positive, happier, spends less time in his room.'

'Good, good. And how's his sleeping? Is he sleeping better? Any more sleepwalking? Bad dreams? According to my notes he hasn't sleepwalked for over eight months.'

'No, Doctor. At least, not to my knowledge.'

'Yes, quite. Well, I am glad things are improving.'

Robbie sat and stared.

Chapter 29

The Holiday

Robbie looked at his mum while she was washing up. He hovered on the threshold to the kitchen.

'Why do we never do anything? We never go away. We used to, but not any more. Not since dad left. I wanna go to the sea.'

Robbie had been thinking about the sea. It had been a year since he had broken his leg. Water had helped such a lot with his recovery. Ever since Patsy had taken him to the Bruce Street baths, he had known water was the key. Well, at least, one of them.

She stopped and looked at him. She was offended.

'But we don't, do we? We never go anywhere!'

'I'm sorry I'm such a bad mother!' His mum was more upset than angry, but it came across as angry.

'I didnae say you were a bad maw.'

'Here! Eat your tea,' she said, slamming a plate of fish fingers and chips down on the table in the lounge.

Later on, Mrs Blair walked into the lounge while Robbie was playing *FIFA*.

'Hey!' she said, trying to get Robbie's attention away from the television screen.

'Hey,' Robbie replied, still playing his game but looking up slightly.

'Maybe you're right. Maybe we don't do anything. Let's go somewhere this weekend. Why don't you bring your friend Jamie?'

Robbie was always thinking. Thinking about football. The comeback. It was never over after all. During his recovery, with Patsy's help, he had worked on his fitness using water – on his strength, his speed, his skills. Over the last six months, he had tried to put in place what he had learned from Patsy Gallacher. He had worked hard on his core strength, waking up early and going through drills in his back garden, and he had worked hard in the pool; his weekly sessions with Jamie were, he believed, really paying off. And, as always, he was working on his football skills by himself and with Jamie and Hamish. But now Robbie wanted to push on even more: 'always go forward!'

He wanted to run. The doctors had warned about the dangers of running on roads. The high impact could lead to further fractures. Robbie had discussed this with Mr McNeil at school. His idea was simple.

'Don't run on roads, then. You've done the right thing running in water. Now push it on. Run on sand, run on grass. Your bones need to be pushed, otherwise they'll nae get stronger. But push them too much and they'll not stand it.'

'So where did you wanna go, Robbie?' Mrs Blair asked.

'Somewhere by the sea. Somewhere with sand. Somewhere with the sun.'

'What? In Scotland? You kidding me?' she replied, laughing.

Robbie, his mum and Jamie left after school on Friday. The drive to Saltcoats took an hour. Robbie googled where they were going and was already planning his training for their time there. He had it mapped out in his head.

Even his mum seemed happier. As they made their way onto the main road, Robbie could see she was smiling. It had been a while, Robbie thought, since he had seen his mum smile. She had a nice smile.

*

When they settled in at the hotel, Robbie looked out of the window towards the beach. It stretched for miles. Robbie couldn't wait to get started. He could smell it – the sea air and the future.

They went for an ice cream and a wander down the main promenade. Robbie kicked a tennis ball as they walked and wove in and out of the street lamps before laying it off to Jamie. There was a slight breeze as they crossed over to the beach and found a place to sit.

'We're going for a paddle, maw,' Robbie declared.

His mum looked younger. Her face looked softer in the sunlight.

When Robbie reached the sea, he felt his toes sink into the ripples of the sand, soft and yielding but also warmly supported. He instantly felt the urge to run, and run he did. He ran through the warm, lapping water. Jamie called after him and followed. The soft sand gave way below his feet with each stride, but the cushioned impact felt good to his legs and invited him to run on faster into the distance. He skipped through the clear, shallow waters, and it felt good – the waters bracing his body and mind, protecting his bones, the shifting but supporting sand beneath his feet, the sun on his back, its refracted rays glistening on the water ahead. Anything was possible. If only he could take this all back with them. Back home.

Chapter 30

Jump!

After school on Monday, Robbie was keen to go and speak to Fred about his weekend away. Robbie strongly felt that water and sand were really going to help him, push him on. He would just have to be more creative in Clydebank…

Fred was sitting hunched in his armchair as normal, looking down. The lounge lit up when Robbie entered, still out of breath from his run. The old ladies who weren't asleep smiled sweetly at Robbie. They liked it when he visited; it was becoming a highlight of the week. It was a lovely spring day and the carers had opened up the double French windows, letting the sunlight beam into the lounge. The sunlight played gently onto Fred's soft but still angular features. Robbie sat down by Fred a little gingerly, feeling awkward, wondering whether Fred was asleep or not. A lady opposite him gave a little wave as she sipped her tea, her knees gripping together as her slumped shoulders rose a little. The television on the wall seemed to be showing a DVD of the same soap as the last time he was here.

Then suddenly, Fred started talking.

'What were the chances of living through this war, Robbie? We didn't have a chance.'

Robbie was confused at first. Fred had never mentioned the war before. Robbie had looked at World War Two at school – Mr McDougal had taught them about it. Robbie quickly tried to do the maths, and worked out that Fred must have been talking about World War Two.

'We travelled down familiar streets on the way to the coast. I must say, Robbie, I took a greater interest in these everyday scenes than normal, thinking I would never see them again. I never felt more proud to be British. I prayed for courage, Robbie. We needed a high tide, a full moon and a clear night. It was all delayed to the sixth of June. Some boys knew they'd never make it. I was scared to death, Robbie. As we felt the Atlantic swelling up, we knew there was no turning back. This was the year 1944. The tide had turned. And there was no going back. The sea was chock-a-block with ships of all shapes and sizes straining at the leash.'

Robbie was trying to piece it together in his head as he listened. Was this Dunkirk? He had definitely learned about that at school. All the ships that Britain could muster were sent over to France to rescue the soldiers. But he wasn't sure, and didn't want to interrupt Fred.

2,000 ships headed to Normandy under the cover of darkness. Dawn. Sixth of June. D-Day.

'And what happened next?' Robbie asked, transfixed by Fred's words and realising at last that it was the D-Day landings that he had been part of. Was still a part of?

Fred looked into the distance as he continued to speak. Robbie followed the line of his vision with his own eyes, but Robbie soon sensed Fred was seeing far beyond the walls of the communal lounge. He was back there.

'Some soldiers argued with each other – they were scared. We all were. Some were seasick, retching over the side. Some, like me, said nothing and looked into the distance from the rails of the ship, shivering, thinking...' Fred's voice trailed off into a soft whisper.

'The transporters cut the engine. We clambered over the railings into the landing craft. The beach was covered with bodies. Men with no legs, no arms. God it was awful, Robbie.'

Robbie Blair sat, perched on the stool next to Fred in the corner of an ordinary-looking room in an ordinary-looking home for ordinary old people. Who knew that Fred was even here? No family to visit him. Who knew what Fred was about to tell him? Was he the first to hear it?

Robbie looked up at Fred.

He looked up and saw the moon. It looked bigger than normal. It was a full, foreboding moon which streaked across the choppy sea in a funnel of light.

'And then?' Robbie asked softly.

'I tried to take myself back, back to the soft summer memories of life on Lord Lovat's estate. But I couldn't stay there for long, I was soon brought back to the horrors of now.'

All was silent as the ships approached land.
The slender but stately figure of Major Lovat stared out, eyes fixed, not blinking. Seagulls weaved and circled the battle turrets of the ship, oblivious. Fred thought of the seagulls back home. What did the seagulls think? What were they seeing?

And then, as the dying gaze of the moon began to move aside and be replaced by the morning light of the sun, the horror of it all began.

Boom. Boom. A torrent of gunfire raged from the ship's rocket launchers, blazing across the sky, showering the beach in the distance, its target the concrete German batteries that fringed the beach. The ship's hull shuddered and creaked with every pounding that was unleashed. It was as if the hull was wincing with pain.

As Fred stared from the ship, he saw the long expanse of beach that signalled the low tide.

'The boffins back home had worked all of this out, of course, Robbie.'

The full moon and the early-rising sun guaranteed the advancing tide –

suitable for landing and taking out the many German water defences – but if they delayed things too long the water would soon be receding again and it would be more dangerous for the soldiers to invade.

Fred knew the hour was approaching when they would be ordered to leave the ship. Major Lovat looked at his men and delivered the command to proceed. In a flurry of activity, the men clambered down the railings and into the landing vessels, which then headed for the beach. The men sat huddled, grasping their guns.

Major Lovat readied himself and, as the drawbridge was launched into the icy waves, jumped first, a giant among men. Others followed in his wake, including a bagpiper wearing a kilt. Yes, a bagpiper! As the man plunged into the water, Fred noticed how he stretched his arms to keep his bagpipes away from the water. Then Fred jumped into the icy cauldron. The coldness of the water cut through to his core but was soon forgotten. It was daylight, 8:20am, but it didn't look like daylight amidst the smoke and fire that swirled around him. As they moved through the water, Fred could feel soldiers drifting past him, into him, already dead. In the distance, Major Lovat skipped through the waves, pushing onwards, as if impervious to all the dangers that surrounded him at every step. And above this pounding, raging inferno the bagpiper's familiar songs could still be heard – loud and proud, weaving through the gunfire like a magical bird.

Bang. He was down. Fred lay on the beach in the wet, sinking sand. Blood pouring into the water, salt water circling the wound. Fred lay there helpless, drowning, as soldiers ran past him, over him, as if he wasn't there. This was it. The end. The gunfire and explosions became fainter, the sand-duned perimeter of the beach retreating with every passing second.

And then it happened. He was back. He was five again. Back on the terraces. With his dad – before the accident. Back in 1925.

Celtic are still looking for that elusive equaliser. Patsy Gallacher lies motionless on the sodden pitch. Young Fred shouts for him to do something. Do something. Jump!

And jump he did. Out of the waves. The waves. Out from death. And onwards. Onwards.

Up on the sand dunes Major Lovat brushed sand from his leather shoes, as if ready to return from a seaside picnic; his curly brown hair danced in the breeze.

'Well, that wasn't too bad, chaps, was it?' he said.

Chapter 31

Hospital Again

When Robbie had to go to the hospital, he was usually conflicted. On the one hand he got to miss school, which was great, obviously, but on the other it was normally another nail in the coffin of his football dream.

He knows how it will pan out. He is in the dreaded room sitting with the doctor, and the conversation is going well, and Robbie is nodding and his mum is nodding, and all the time Robbie is waiting, waiting for the 'f'-word to come up: yes, football. Robbie knows it is coming. Waiting there, seeing all the goals he was going to score, all the dizzying runs past defenders, all the caps he would have earned for Celtic and Scotland.

And then the doctor will say, 'So obviously you still can't play football, Robbie.' He will say other things after that, but Robbie will block them out. Robbie is out of there, has left the building, is running around Clydebank, exercising, machining himself into the supreme footballer.

'Robbie! Will you get out of bed? We'll be late!'

On the train there, Robbie thought about things. He had broken his leg eighteen months ago. Since then, so much had happened. His meetings with Patsy Gallacher: although he had been there, even he didn't know what they were – were they real? Were they a dream? And if he told anyone…what would be the point? No one would believe him.

But with every run, every drill, every session, he had stopped worrying about what the meetings were. What did it matter? It mattered that Patsy Gallacher had come into his life, in whatever form, and had started the whole process. Life, he was beginning to realise, was all about moments – moments stitched together. And it didn't matter, really, where those moments happened. Just *when* they happened.

There were some delays during the train journey, and Robbie's mum began to be worried about being late for the appointment. Robbie sank into the tartan pile of the train seat and looked out at the conveyor belt of back gardens that streamed past. He liked to do this on train journeys – imagining the lives of the people who lived in those houses. They all had their stories to tell. What would someone whizzing past his small, nondescript back garden think up for him? Would they even come close?

As they walked into the Victorian hospital, Robbie was transported back to the world of broken bones, and he steeled himself.

The corridor was really busy and there was an ever-flowing wave of human traffic in all lanes. Never one to miss an opportunity, Robbie took out his battered tennis ball and weaved his way through the stream of people, the ball seemingly stuck to his feet. His mum told him to stop, but he was oblivious. A male doctor smiled at him from above his clipboard.

In the waiting room, Robbie noticed a boy sitting across from him. Robbie remembered him from the last time he had broken his leg, and also from when he had been in hospital to receive treatment. Fraser – that was it, Robbie remembered. Both boys recognised each other. But there was a difference. Robbie felt strong and fitter than ever and was, though he would deny it, running and playing football again – even if it was largely by himself. Fraser, by contrast, stood next to his mum with a cast on his leg. They were the same age and had been on the same treatment since they had both broken their legs. But here was Robbie, fighting fit, and there was Fraser, back like he was before. Fraser shrugged politely at

Robbie. Robbie wondered why, if their stories were so similar, they were on different pages now. Robbie thought he knew.

After a short wait, Robbie and his mum were shown into Dr Hergler's office. It was the same as always, Robbie thought as he quickly looked around, surveying the scene.

'So, Robbie, how have you been generally?'

Robbie's mum nodded, as always, for Robbie.

'Okay,' Robbie said, giving nothing away to anyone, as usual. Get through this – say what you have to say.

'So for eighteen months now you have been visiting us twice a year and receiving infusions of Zoledronate. Well, the good news is, according to your latest scan, your bone density has increased by two points, which is pleasing, and unusual.'

Pleasing, Robbie thought. It's great. That means football, surely. Perhaps Robbie could go legit and admit he had been training himself for football again.

'You are still exercising a lot, I see, which is good for you. All weight-bearing non-contact. Just don't go mad.'

Don't go mad. Robbie thought: Going mad is what makes you great. What did he know?

Then there was a pause. Robbie felt what was coming: this was it. His green and blue eyes then fixed Dr Hergler, who coughed. Would he remember the script? Would he keep to it? Robbie stared again. Or would he change?

'Obviously you're not playing football. You're not playing football, are you?' said the doctor, looking over his spectacles.

Robbie felt cornered, confined. He felt his mum's eyes boring into him from the side.

'No, Doctor,' his mum nodded with a smile that Robbie knew wasn't a smile.

'Good,' the doctor replied, looking at his computer while Robbie continued to stare, unmoved.

Chapter 32

Training

When Robbie woke up on that spring morning, the sunlight drifted through his window and into his eyes. He decided in a moment what was going to change. He would play football again. Soon. He was ready; the training he had been doing with Patsy and the training he had been doing by himself and with Jamie was starting to pay off. The plan – strength, speed, skills – was working. He hadn't rushed things. The plan was a plan, not a momentary change of thought or a whim. It was a plan.

Now the time was right to turn out for training with the school team. He just had to do it without his mum knowing. He knew what she would say.

Robbie packed his boots and kit, buried them really deep in his rucksack, folded neatly, concealed like his dreams.

As Maths finished and his classmates quickly ran out to play, Robbie delayed following them, pretending to finish off something in his book, waiting for Mr McDougal to return to class after disappearing into the cupboard. It was all about timing, and Robbie did timing well. That's what waiting and dreaming does: it helps with timing, because you've already been there – a thousand times.

'Mr McDougal…' Robbie ambled in as Mr McDougal shuffled pieces of paper together and put them in a file.

'Robbie, how can I help you?'

'I want to play football for the team again,' Robbie said, coming straight out with it.

Mr McDougal looked at him.

'But you can't, Robbie. Your bones. Your mum's told us. You told us.'

'But I'm getting stronger and fitter. And I'm faster than anyone. If you don't get tackled you'll nae be hurt, Mr McDougal.'

'That's good, Robbie. That's really good. I'm glad, I really am. But no one can avoid tackles. Forever. It's impossible. Now, out you go to play. And, Robbie – you're not training in the middle of the night any more, are you?'

'I don't need to do that now,' Robbie replied, staring back at his teacher.

'Okay,' Mr McDougal said as Robbie left the classroom.

Robbie was dressed in his kit when his mum arrived at home from work. He was sitting in the lounge, waiting.

'Hi, Robbie,' she said, rushing past, not even noticing he was in his kit. 'I've got loads to do. And what a day at work! The new boss has started and the girls aren't happy with what they've seen. What do you fancy for tea? I think we've just got fish fingers left,' she called out from the kitchen.

'Maw, I wanna play football again.'

'Yes, we've fish fingers,' she said, carrying on looking into the freezer. 'What did you say?'

'I said I wanna play football again!'

The noises stopped in the kitchen and Robbie's mum came marching through.

'No, Robbie! Absolutely not!' Mrs Blair shouted, suddenly looking stern.

'But I'm stronger now and faster, and it's been way over a year.'

Robbie was overcome with the idea that she was wrong. But he knew he had to try a different way. He knew what his mum was like.

'But what if I went and did the running part, the skills part, and then when they play games, I'll watch? I won't take part in that part, I promise,' Robbie pleaded.

'No, Robbie. I know what you're like. Absolutely not. Now that's it finished. Let me make the tea.'

'But that's not fair. You're so mean! You won't even let me try!' And with that, Robbie ran up to his room. His eyes welled up. He lay on his side and cried into his Celtic pillow. He didn't even think of football this time. What was the point?

Chapter 33

The Letter

When Robbie woke up, it suddenly hit him. He knew how to get to go to training! It was obvious, in a way. But sometimes the most obvious plans are the best, and as usual sleep had provided the answer. Robbie Blair had another plan.

Mrs Blair was rushing around as normal, a flurry of stress and exasperation.

'Will ye get a move on, Robbie? What are you even doing? Will you come and get your cereal, and stop watching TV? *Please!*'

Robbie came through to the kitchen and quietly took his bowl of corn flakes. He sat at the small table and thought. Waited. Timing. As his mum ran upstairs to dry her hair and get herself ready for work, Robbie put his spoon down and got a piece of paper out of his rucksack, which was by the back door.

It read:

Dear Mr McDougal,
I give permission to my son Robbie Blair to take part in school football training, as long as the activities are non-contact. He is allowed to do the following:

General running
Jumping
Football skills/drills
He is not allowed to do the following:
Taking part in actual games
Tackling
Thanks a lot,

After re-reading the letter, Robbie folded it neatly so that most of the content was obscured from his mum. He handed it to his mum alongside the reading section of his home-school book.

Good thinking, he thought. A pile of things to sign off – just what she wanted when she was in a rush. Get her just before they were about to leave the house. Just before.

Robbie deliberately made himself late, delaying everything that he was late doing anyway.

'Get changed, take your bowl through, have you nae cleaned your teeth yet? Are you on a go-slow today?'

It was working, Robbie thought.

And then, just as they were about to leave: bingo!

'Sorry, maw, I forgot. Can you sign this, please?' Robbie said politely, offering his home-school book. 'For my reading.'

'Where? Okay,' she said, rushing.

'And this.' Robbie put the letter in front of his mum. She enlarged her eyes in an irritated fashion.

'It's for swimming. Permission,' Robbie said, not blinking, trying not to show any particular facial expression at all.

'Done. Now come on, we are leaving,' Mrs Blair said, quickly signing the form.

Robbie put the form and book in his rucksack. Job done.

After tea Robbie announced to his mum that he was going out.

'I'm going out with Hamish to the park.'

'Don't be late back.'

Robbie shut the door and quickly ran off to the John Brown football pitches, where the team were practising. It had gone as planned.

When Robbie arrived, Hamish quickly spotted him.

'You made it, then?'

Mr McDougal came over, wearing a tracksuit and retro-looking football boots.

'Robbie! What brings you here?' he said, looking confused. Robbie was ready and gave him the letter, which he quickly read.

'Are you sure? Is your maw sure?'

'Aye, she's sure, just no games,' said Robbie confidently.

'Okay,' he said, folding the letter and putting it in his back pocket.

The session was divided up into different sections: warm-up, some speed work, some skills, shooting practice and games. Stuart, the caretaker, used to be in the RAF and clearly enjoyed the physical aspects of training. Lots of the exercises were ones that Robbie had learned from Patsy and that he practised himself on a daily basis. The children were told to do the plank, a favourite of Robbie's which Patsy had taught him at John Brown's Shipyard. Robbie loved the plank. On his early morning runs, he always finished off with the plank, in the wastelands under the shadow of the Titan. The plank summed up much of his vision – stay strong, be determined.

The planks on evidence at tonight's training were nothing to shout about, Robbie thought. They started off poor and got poorer. Saggy bottoms, arched backs and, even worse – cheating. The plank, for Robbie, held an almost religious significance, so to see the giggling numpties not taking it seriously, dipping in and out of it, pained him. Robbie's planks were straight, solid and unwavering, his face unmoved by pain.

'You can stop now, Robbie,' Stuart said, crouching down by him so Robbie could process what he was saying.

'You're strong, Robbie. You're still small, but very strong,' Stuart continued.

'Thanks,' Robbie said.

As Robbie pulled himself up, he saw a thickset boy with dark brown hair smirk at him.

'Hey you! Strong man. You think you're something special, don't you? Special needs, more like! Good luck in the game,' he sneered, giving Robbie a thumbs up. Kyle Ferguson. He had always hated Kyle. A bully, Robbie had always thought, and Robbie was rarely wrong about such things.

The lanky frame of Mr McDougal came over to the boys.

'I won't be playing in the game. I can't,' Robbie replied, and as he said it, he knew it was the wrong thing to say.

'Ah, diddums, poor Robbie cannae even play football at football training. What's the point in you even being here?' sneered Kyle.

Robbie stared at him. But left him alone. This time.

When it was time for games, Robbie moved over to the sideline. He could see what Mr McDougal was going to say but was ready to step aside anyway. Retreat to the shadows.

Robbie practised some skills for a while and took some free kicks on a neighbouring pitch and did some crossbar challenges. But then, for the second half, he came back to the sideline and watched. Robbie watched without taking too much in. He had trained himself to do it. If he watched too intently, he would get too worked up about what he was missing. Looking, not watching. He was good at watching, but sometimes, for his own sake, he just looked.

He suddenly realised Stuart was coming over to him. 'Robbie, I've just had a wee word with Mr McDougal and we were discussing whether we could get you involved in a game.'

'A game! Are you serious?'

'Well, on account of your bones you cannae be tackled, obviously. So maybe if you stood out a bit. Then it wouldnae happen.'

'Stood out?' Some would take Stuart's comment as a compliment, but Robbie smelt a rat.

Stuart went on. 'Aye – if you wore a different coloured bib to everyone else, then everyone would know not to tackle you.'

He produced a pink bib awkwardly.

'Pink! Are you for real?'

'I'll admit the colour's no' the best. It's all we've got. But at least you'll be playing, Robbie.'

Robbie gave it some thought. It was a game, after all. All he had been dreaming of.

'Let's do it,' he said, putting the bib on and walking onto the pitch.

Robbie may as well have had a neon light on him saying, 'Look at me, I'm a wee jessie!'

Robbie played for a while and did some nice tricks, but it just didn't feel right. It flickered into his head to say he was feeling sick and to go back to the sidelines. But Robbie Blair wasn't the quitting kind. So he stuck it out.

Kyle came up to him at the end. 'Nice bib, strong man! And' — pointing at Robbie's Celtic top— 'if you're such a big fan, what's with the blue eye? Have you got a secret love for Rangers?'

Robbie clenched his fist, but something inside him stopped him. Jamie called over to him, and Robbie went.

Chapter 34

Ryan

At school the next day, after PE Mr McNeil walked over to Robbie.

'I saw you yesterday, Robbie.'

Robbie looked up. 'What d'you mean?'

'I saw you at football training.'

'Oh, okay.'

'Was that your first game back?'

'Aye.'

'You looked strong. Fit. You must have been pleased.'

'Aye, I think so.'

'You think so? You sure about that?' Mr McNeil laughed as he stroked the fashionable stubble on his face. 'How long's it been, Robbie, since you last broke a bone?'

'Eighteen months, more or less,' Robbie replied.

'And how have you been getting strong? How have you been doing it?'

Robbie stopped kicking his tennis ball and looked at him. 'I woke up one day and decided that if I didn't do something different I wasnae gonna play football again. Only I was going to change what the doctors said. I was going to make myself stronger, faster than anyone. I met someone too. A footballer. There was no one stronger or faster. And after I met him, I knew what I had to do. I had to think differently. To everyone else. Even to myself.'

'That's brilliant, Robbie. And I think I can help you get even faster and stronger. I run some fitness classes at Clydebank High. I think they could really help you.'

Chapter 35

Forward

After Maths, Robbie suddenly decided he wanted to talk to Mr McDougal. The other children filtered out of class, but Robbie hovered around Mr McDougal's desk.

'Mr McDougal, I need to speak to you.'

Mr McDougal put his work down on the desk and looked at Robbie. 'Okay, Robbie. Tell me.'

'Well, it's difficult to say, but I'll just say it anyway. When I kept breaking bones – well, certainly when I broke my last bone…well, I saw a face. I have no idea where it came from. But it spoke to me. And then this face became a person that visited me and sort of coached me. And maybe, just maybe, this might have been Patsy Gallacher. I don't know.'

Mr McDougal gazed at Robbie. 'Patsy Gallacher? My all-time favourite Celt! Are you winding me up, Robbie?'

'No. That's it, that's it. That's what happened.'

'And is this why you're running around late at night?'

'Maybe. I'm not sure. I'm not making anything up.'

Mr McDougal stared at him. 'Have you told your maw?'

'What do you think? You know what she would say. What would anyone say?'

And with that, Robbie walked towards the classroom door.

'But, Mr McDougal…'

'Yes, Robbie?'

'I will be a footballer again. I will make it.'

Robbie left the classroom while Mr McDougal continued to gaze into the distance.

Later on that night, after tea, Robbie announced he was going for a run.

'Well, okay. But no more than an hour. And don't do anything stupid!'

Mrs Blair carried on looking at the TV when she answered, which Robbie thought was a good sign she was coming around to his thinking. Even if she didn't know about the football. Yet.

Robbie, ever the planner, had calculated that it would take him ten minutes to run to Mr McNeil's fitness class, thirty minutes to do the class and ten minutes to run back. According to his plan he would even have time for ten minutes recovery!

When Robbie arrived at Clydebank High, he was a little unsure about where to go, and became a little anxious that he was going to miss the class. Luckily, a caretaker drifted into view, walking past Robbie in his old-fashioned overalls. He was a small, wiry man and he had a drill in his hand.

'Can I help you, young man?' he asked.

'I'm looking for the fitness classes. With, erm, Mr McNeil. I mean Ryan.'

'Aye. Are you Robbie?' the old man asked.

'Aye!' Robbie replied.

'Just over there and to the left. Give it your best,' replied the caretaker as he drifted away again.

Chapter 36

Achnacarry

This week was the week of the Primary 7 trip to Achnacarry Outward Bound centre.

Robbie's class set off before school started. Robbie hadn't slept the night before; he was far too excited. When he arrived at school, the big bus stood there ready. Archie McDingle arrived with about three suitcases and a fussing mother. Mr McDougal stood at the entrance to the bus, welcoming the children on and easing the worries of the parents. Robbie went for his normal middle position on the bus and sat next to Hamish, as always.

Robbie fell asleep for most of the journey, but woke up as the bus was veering into Achnacarry. The bus wound its way over a stone bridge and then along a meandering road that was flanked by trees on either side. Once through this, like a channel being tuned in, they could see the snow-capped hills and mountains surrounding Achnacarry. Robbie remembered Fred telling him that he had come here when he was a young man – it was where he had been trained. What would Fred have thought when he arrived here?

'Greeted with hills, rivers, mountains. The scenery hit us right in the eye, Robbie!'

On the first day, there was an assault course. Everyone got completely covered in mud but, despite this, they all thought it was amazing. Mr McDougal thought that everyone would be exhausted and too tired to stay up late talking in their dormitories. But he was wrong, and had to go in several times and do his 'stern teacher' thing. Secretly though, he could understand their excitement – for most, it was their first taste of true independence. For Robbie, it felt like an extension of what he had been doing for over a year.

On the second day, there was an orienteering course through the surrounding forest. Greg, the instructor divided up the class into five groups of pupils, all with the target of reaching a waterfall in the middle of the forest before anyone else. Robbie's group decided to split up.

But suddenly, Robbie was alone. Too alone.

'Callum! Hamish!' Robbie called out across the forest. But he heard nothing except the incessant rain, which pounded down on the trees above. Just then, there was a sudden movement in the distance. A flicker of colour, a shape. What was it? One of the team? He called out again. It was no one. Then again: a snap of branches, a piece of bark breaking, footsteps. An echo. Ah, a deer. He could see it now. No problem.

Robbie walked on through the forest. He continued to shout to his friends, but heard nothing. Then came another sound. Water. Was this the waterfall they were meant to find? A trickle was all he heard at first, but with every step the sound grew louder.

Robbie looked keenly ahead of him and to the side and behind him, trying to find a trace, a glimmer of where he was meant to be going: the path. Something drew him on in his current direction, though, if anything, the trees were getting denser, the view becoming less clear. There was one thing, though: Robbie noticed that, as he clambered stealthily through the trees, whenever he slipped on loose uneven soil, whenever he tripped on a jutting branch he hadn't seen, he was able to adjust his change of direction with lightning speed. As he became more confident, he found himself forgetting that he was lost from the group, and instead lost himself in the ever-changing world, bobbing and weaving through its natural defences with grace and ease.

But all dizzying runs come to an end. The trees had become so dense that Robbie could barely see in front of him, but he could hear the water, louder now, and knew the instructor had said the finishing point was by the waterfall. Robbie saw a boulder in front of him and took the opportunity to vault over it like a stag. As he landed and prepared to run again, eyes looking forward, his foot tripped over a branch that was sticking out from a fallen tree. Robbie fell, and even Robbie Blair could not keep his balance this time. He tumbled into the trees, and continued to fall further. He slid and tumbled through an opening in the trees and must have fallen about ten to twelve feet in all. Robbie instinctively grabbed out at branches that he could see rushing past him, but it was happening all too quickly.

And then he came to rest. Dazed and confused, he lay there for a few seconds. And then it hit him: the sound of a waterfall. From the rocky ledge where he had come to rest, Robbie saw the gushing rapids streaming down in front of him, blasting their way down over the rocks with impressive power. He also felt the waterfall; it hung in the air like an icy cloud, sometimes touching his face.

Robbie stood up and looked around him. What was he to do next? He looked up. He had dropped quite a height and it would be difficult to climb back from where he had fallen. And indeed, he thought, what would be the point? Robbie suddenly thought of a book he had read in Reception: 'Can't go over it, can't go under it, got to go through it!' But Robbie was going over it.

He stared across the gushing rapids that were flowing down below him with crazy speed. It was quite a drop down to the waterfall, and quite a stretch to the other side. Jumping was an option, but the challenge was made more difficult because there was, literally, no room for him to run at it. It was just too far. And how would he land? And where? Through the hanging mist, he could see quite a big boulder jutting out of the water. If he could only reach it! But he thought the water itself looked deep in places and swirled around like a whirlpool at times.

Robbie thought. This was another moment. He thought hard. And then a voice cut through over the crashing waters below.

'Jump!' it said.

Robbie looked quickly at the man. He was dressed in green military uniform. He had a beret on, and Robbie could see that he had a rifle strapped to his back. What was he doing here?

'Jump!' he said again. Robbie looked at the man, whose angular features had remained fixed, unmoving.

So Robbie bent his knees as if he was doing a fitness class with Ryan, straightened his arms back and braced himself for flight. Just before he jumped he glanced at the figure again, but it had gone as quickly as it had appeared. A kingfisher sat perched on an overhanging branch, watching on.

Robbie flew from the ledge over the misty, roaring waters. He seemed to be in the air for an eternity, and his eyes widened as he soaked up the wind, the air, the danger of it all. As he flew through the air, he was joined in flight by the electric blue of the kingfisher. He landed twelve feet below on the other side of the stream. He landed on the boulder perfectly. Easy knees, the softest landing you could imagine. A perfect ten. Even the kingfisher looked impressed.

Now just to wait for the others, Robbie thought.

Chapter 37

Back Again!

When Robbie returned home, he was exhausted.

'I feel like I'm going to sleep for a week, but it was great, maw!'

'That's good, love. But I hope you didnae do anything risky!' she said, unpacking his muddy clothes.

As Robbie lay in bed, he knew he couldn't sleep for long. His long-awaited return to match football was in two days' time.

'Are you sure you're ready for this? Today?' Mr McDougal asked as he swept leaves away from the entrance to the school gates.

Robbie stopped running and flicked the tennis ball up into his hand.

'Yeah, yeah.'

'Does your maw know you're playing?' Mr McDougal asked, his arms folded, suddenly looking more serious.

'Maybe,' Robbie lied.

At this point a stream of children traipsed past, their giggling drowning out Mr McDougal's words.

'And the doctors?'

'I canna hear you. See you later!' Robbie shouted out. But he had heard. Quickly putting away Mr McDougal's questions into a drawer that he rarely used but knew was there, he went about his normal school business.

The referee blew. Scott tapped the ball to Robbie and, even though the game had just begun, Robbie only had one thing on his mind. He skipped past the first opponent as he normally did, without thinking, and then onto the next. A ginger-haired boy shoulder-barged Robbie. Robbie pushed him back, and the boy fell over. The referee looked, but then said: 'Play on.' Robbie felt good.

A nondescript game in most respects; the wind blew hard, and some of the players were regretting not putting their base layers on. Robbie wasn't wearing a base layer, but he wasn't complaining either. In fact, since he had been taking freezing cold showers on a daily basis, he didn't seem to feel the cold. He'd read about some player from the 80s who, after recovering from injury, used to bathe in ice, and Robbie decided he would do the same. His mum thought he was mad.

The referee blew for the second half. Hamilton kicked off and played it back to their central midfielder, a tall boy with slicked-back brown hair. From there they played a long, looping ball which was headed away by Hamish, who was covering to his left. Unfortunately, the ball landed in the path of a speeding Hamilton winger, who launched the ball past the defender, knowing that he would have the pace to pass Hamish, meet up with the ball and have time to think about his next moment. The ball continued to roll, and just at the point where it seemed to go out, the winger rescued it and 'Cruyff turned' it back into the action.

Meanwhile, Hamish had recovered enough to sprint back to his defensive position. The winger nutmegged Hamish, embarrassing him once more, and then chipped the ball into the eighteen-yard box. It landed perfectly for the Hamilton striker, who hit a thunderous half-volley. The Clydebank parents, fearing the worst, watched on as the goalie bravely stuck his head in the way. But, to the horror of the Clydebank fans, the ball bounced off his head – while leaving him seemingly unconscious on the ground – and rolled dangerously towards the goal line. The tension built; everybody could feel it. The ball crept closer to the line and the Clydebank players froze with fear. Out of the blue and out of the green, Robbie Blair flew in with the speed of a train and hooked the ball away on the line. Clydebank was saved.

With five minutes to go, the Hamilton keeper kicked the ball out. It was brought down by one of the Hamilton players. Robbie Blair smashed into him with enough strength to push the boy over, but not enough to attract the gaze of the referee. Play on. Robbie rushed to the ball in time to play it back across to Jamie, who placed it neatly into the net.

Chapter 38

Cathkin Together

'We've got two weeks until the semi-final!' Robbie said to Callum on their way home from school. They were pleased it was the weekend.

'Let's train at Cathkin tomorrow! We can bring Jamie too! Make some sandwiches, get the train. Saturday sorted.'

The friends agreed – it was the perfect plan. And Robbie still couldn't believe it. Robbie Blair in a semi-final.

Getting off at Crosshill Station, the friends turned left and made the short walk down Cathcart Road, turning left for Cathkin Park. They could have stayed left, passed the pavilion, walked past the jagged remains of the old entrance gate, down the empty space which was formerly occupied by the old grandstand. But they didn't. Robbie preferred to take them the way he remembered it – at least, the way he thought he remembered it. It had been a while. So, up the bank over the wooden steps, through the curtain of ash trees and then…Cathkin! It looked just as it had always done. A green stage ready to be explored by the assembled actors. This time without Patsy.

They went through a series of drills, shapes and set plays. Robbie had become quite the expert on scenarios that might pan out at any time and on ways to cope with them. It was all those nights of thinking, dreaming, wishing. What else could you do when you couldn't sleep?

At about 3:30pm, the light changed. It started to become dark, and stillness gripped the air.

'Of course!' said Hamish, who knew about such things – he liked science, was good at it. Mr McDougal always looked to him when he wanted a question answered correctly.

He went on, 'It's a solar eclipse! Mr McDougal talked about it at school on Friday. When the moon blocks out the light from the sun. Like this.' He helpfully demonstrated this for his friends with a football and a tennis ball.

'Where's the Earth?' Jamie asked.

'That's us,' said Robbie. 'We are the Earth. At least, that's where I live. Most of the time.'

And then it happened. It went darker still. And it felt bad. Like something really bad was going to happen. Maybe there were clues in the sky. Maybe those books were right all along.

The Sun was largely eclipsed by now and had turned into a strange dark sphere, save for a few shards of light yet to be engulfed. Robbie looked around. The dog walker, the dog, his two friends had all become, curiously, with no sun, shadows in the dusky light.

And then more shadows slipped out from the trees and onto the pitch. A whistle piercing the darkness. The thump of a ball, heavier than normal, flying through the air, which was curiously both dark and light.

'Give it to Patsy!' came a shout from the darkness.

Robbie watched as the small dark figure caught the ball effortlessly with his foot and made his way through the darkness, weaving his path with a supernatural flair.

The old grandstand is full, and sudden bursts of flashlight punctuate the air – the photographers and journalists alive to the importance of the occasion. A sea of steel-capped boots tramples the ashen steps of the surrounding terraces. All eyes on Patsy. He dances through defender after defender in the fading light and delivers another precision cross to Jimmy McGrory's head, which propels the ball into the top corner of the net. For a moment he thinks about the magic of tonight.

The unfurling smoke and fire of Dixon's Blazers streak across the bleak sky, beacons of light on this strangest of nights. A rolling clap of thunder, the whistle again and then more. The jolt of the rivet gun, the clank of the anvil, and the echo of a thousand boots marching to war and never coming back.

And now lightning.

It lit the whole of Cathkin Park in a moment. Every kick. Every face. Every thought. Every dream. Caught, paused and saved. Ready to be discovered again.

Chapter 39

Dad

Robbie was running to school. Standard. Skipping past defenders and waiting for the goalkeeper to make his move by the school gates.

'Robbie!' A voice came from the roof of the school. A thin, dark-haired, rough-looking man in a hi-vis vest, on his knees.

'Robbie!' he repeated. 'It's me, your dad.'

I know who you are, Robbie thought.

He went on, 'I'm doing some work on the school roof.'

'I can see,' Robbie said, squinting up at the crouched figure.

'I hear you're playing football again?'

'Aye, sort of.'

'Well, okay. Say hello to your maw for me.'

'Aye,' Robbie muttered. He would be the last person she would be interested in hearing from, he thought.

After school, Robbie ran to the field behind his house with Hamish for a kick about.

'Look!' Hamish said.

'What?'

'It's your dad again,' Hamish said. 'He's coming over.'

Robbie's heart dropped. The feeling you should get when your dad comes over to collect you or see you after a while – he didn't get that. That had gone. He just feared the worst. And he was normally right.

'So, how's the football?' his dad asked. He was dressed in stonewashed jeans and a battered leather jacket, but still had his hi-vis vest on over the top.

Robbie smelt drink; he smelt fags and beer. That smell. The smell of the pub. He had smelt it when he was younger too, but he didn't know what it was then.

'Alreet?' he drawled.

Robbie's dad grabbed the ball from Hamish and swerved drunkenly into the middle of the pitch. Then he turned round and, facing the two children, ran at them with a new sense of purpose. Close to Robbie, he looked him in the eyes. 'Watch and learn, son, watch and learn.'

Robbie could remember him saying things like that when he was younger. He'd thought he was funny then.

'Just like the old days, Robbie, me and you in the park!' his dad continued.

Attempting a step over, his wayward boot circled around the ball, clumsily forgetting its purpose, and then he fell to the ground in a pathetic fall.

Hamish laughed nervously, but then stopped.

Robbie stood over him. Stood over his dad, looking down.

He looked at him, and he looked at him real hard. And then he stopped looking at him, because he didn't have to look at him any more. Because he knew.

'You're embarrassing,' Robbie said.

Robbie's dad looked at him, pale, broken in his own way. 'What d'you mean by that?' he said defensively and a touch aggressively.

Robbie continued to look down at his dad. 'You've always been crap and you carry on being crap. That's it. We're done.'

With that, Robbie and his friend took their ball and walked away back to Robbie's house. Hamish turned round and saw Robbie's dad stagger to his feet, shake the grass cuttings from his clothes and then walk the other way. Again.

Chapter 40

Flowers

Robbie ran to the home after school. He was desperate to speak to Fred after visiting Cathkin Park. Again. He was also keen to speak to Fred about the presentation he had to make for his final year assembly at primary school.

He weaved in and out of the lamp posts with his tennis ball, down the Dumbarton Road, skipping past people on the pavement who were caught up in his 'game'. Robbie never went anywhere without his tennis ball. Or without running. It was like his religion. The lamp posts became his cones – he was sprinting between them, then walking, then slowing down, then stopping. Then repeat. He was definitely using everything around him.

'Use what you've got!' he said.

Turning into the cul-de-sac where the home was, Robbie stopped. Fred was there, watering the flowers in the baskets hanging outside the home. Robbie had never seen Fred standing up, mainly because he was old, but also because he only had one leg. Robbie was impressed but then confused. He's always slouched on a chair, he thought. How is he up? As Robbie ran to the entrance, he slowed down, and at that moment Fred looked up from the tub of petunias he was watering.

'How you doing?' Fred said. He was taller, less hunched than Robbie imagined he would be standing up. His eyes were still clear and bright, as always. His skin was less creased in the soft after-school sunlight.

He winked at Robbie.

'Have you been looking for me?' Fred said. 'Or have I been looking for you?' he continued.

Robbie looked and said, 'Aye, I think.' He squinted in the sunlight.

Fred stood strong and tall. 'Keep believing, Robbie. Keep believing.'

As Robbie took these words in, one of the health assistants arrived for work. Robbie knew her from his previous visits.

She guided Robbie in; she didn't bother signing him in today.

'I'm real sorry, Robbie,' she said. Robbie was confused. What did she mean? Why was she sorry? What had happened? Robbie ran home.

Chapter 41

The Video

Everyone was sitting in the school hall, looking at the empty stage. A few late parents, probably stuck in traffic, meandered apologetically through the aisles of people, looking for solitary, elusive seats. The adults towered over the tiny seats that were laid out in neat rows across the hall. It was the end of the summer term. The P7 assembly. The last hurrah before departing for the scary corridors of Clydebank High School. There was a buzz in the hall, a lively mix of happiness and sadness, moments gone but remembered, shared, moments to come, moments forgotten – unless you were there.

The children had worked hard all term on their various projects. A mixture of comedy skits, dance routines, karaoke, some 'impressions' and acts that were hard to categorise!

Robbie's mum was one of the latecomers. She was owed some time from the factory and was able to have a couple of hours off mid-morning. She was one of the last ones to arrive. There had been some kind of issue to help sort out – a dispute over pay at the depot. There was always something. She was stressed, as always, and her forehead glowed as she lowered herself down onto her seat. She scanned the hall for Robbie, eventually seeing him at the side of the stage towards the back of the hall. She waved at him in that over-the-top way that parents do at shows like this. He gave her an awkward wave and an awkward smile. But he was glad she had arrived. Now the factory was gone, the petty dispute finished with, the traffic gone. Just Robbie and the school, the school hall. Here.

Mr McDougal walked onto the stage. His hair was a little curlier now, Robbie thought, and a little greyer – maybe the stress of the outward bound trip to Achnacarry. He had a clipboard with notes, which he held to his chest as he talked.

'So, welcome. Welcome for the last time. Unfortunately, Mrs McClusky couldn't be here today, but, as the support act, so to speak, she's asked me to headline. But, of course, the true headliners are you lot – right there! The last leg of the journey that we have all been on together for the past seven years.

'I remember you all as wee bairns arriving at four years of age, scared little rabbits in the headlights, about to start school for the first time, worrying about what lay ahead. I've watched you all grow and flourish and turn into the outstanding individuals that I see now, waiting for the next leg of the journey to begin. Perhaps scared, perhaps excited, maybe a mixture of both.'

Mr McDougal's eyes began to fill up. He brushed his eyes with his finger and breathed in.

'So here we are. No more from me. Let us begin.'

Mr McDougal sat down, and the lights dimmed.

Charlotte McCall stood up, took a deep breath, and then, in clipped, precise tones, introduced the acts. Mrs Blair laughed to herself. Why, she was twice poor Robbie's height, she thought. Was he really going to Clydebank High School in a few weeks? He looked so small sitting there with his friends.

'First up we have Cameron and Callum's juggling act.'

This was hilarious, but it wasn't meant to be. The boys had practised hard, but nerves and juggling are a dangerous mix. Starting with four balls, the balls went everywhere – under seats, under the stage. The boys spent more time on their knees searching for the balls than actually juggling. The parents laughed, not because they were being unkind, but because it was impossible not to. Downgrading their ambitions to three balls didn't help matters. Then down to two. Still no success. Red-faced, the boys were now down to one ball. Robbie whispered to Hamish, 'Technically this is a game of catch now.' Cameron threw the ball, and it took an eternity to arc across the hall to his friend. Miraculously, Callum caught it. The hall erupted into applause. There was warmth in the room.

They were a hard act to follow. Some slick traditional dancing followed, then various pop song renditions, some comedy acts and even a little magic. Hamish did some impressions of his teachers that were actually very good. Robbie enjoyed Hamish's act, especially his impression of the school secretary, Mrs Mackintosh. But then it dawned on him that he was next, and – which was worse – last. He needed the large interactive white board that formed the backdrop to the stage. Mr McDougal clicked on the laptop and Robbie climbed up onto the stage.

'And, last on, we have Robbie Blair, who has made a presentation about the famous Celtic footballer, Patsy Gallacher.'

Robbie had worked hard on the presentation. He talked through Patsy's early life, moving to Clydebank when he was a small boy, talked about how Patsy had run his school football team while in primary school due to lack of adult interest and how, though his team won the cup, they weren't allowed to receive it because they were managed by a child.

Robbie stopped for a moment. His football shirt. From the church. Hidden under his bed. Was it possible?

Mr McDougal noticed Robbie was lost for words and asked him if he was all right.

It was as if someone had pressed pause. Robbie looked out onto the sea of faces. Mr McDougal's voice became deep and distant, swirling around the room.

'Are you okay, Robbie?'

A small boy in an old football shirt stood on the stage, pale and slight, looking at him.

'Are you okay, Robbie?' he asked again.

And then, as if his head had been dragged from a freezing pool of water, Robbie was back in the hall, the faces ready for his next words.

Robbie took a deep breath and continued. He talked through Patsy's move to Celtic, and reeled out all the impressive stats about Patsy's record.

'He went on to play for Celtic for fifteen years from 1911 to 1925, featuring in 491 games in all competitions. In 464 games in major competitions, Patsy scored 192 goals. Today he ranks as Celtic's sixth-highest goal scorer, behind Jimmy McGrory, Bobby Lennox, Henrik Larsson, Stevie Chalmers and Jimmy Quinn.'

Grandparents in the audience nodded proudly as details of Patsy's impressive career were shared. Robbie also included some details of Patsy's time at John Brown's Shipyard, where he was once fined six pounds for arriving late for his shift. Robbie explained that there was no real footage of Patsy playing, but by all accounts he was one of the best players to ever play the game. And then, of course, the famous 1925 Patsy Gallacher Cup Final. With that Goal. Moments gone. But still here. He knew. He understood his tricks, the dinks, the stops, the drag backs and his strength.

But all the people in the hall had were the faded photos on the screen and Robbie's words. To finish, Robbie played a clip he had been able to find which showed Celtic (and Patsy Gallacher) running out onto the pitch, triumphant, after edging the same famous cup final 21. Mr McDougal clicked 'play'. Would it work? Yes! It began to play, and Robbie turned to watch the flickering images of the crowd at the Scottish Cup Final, Hampden Park, in 1925.

A sea of caps and hats stretched to the sky, as if the ground itself was made of people. Then the sprightly players made their way breezily down through a channel in the crowd, down the steps and onto the pitch, holding the trophy aloft. One by one, the players, in their big white flapping shorts. Some with shirts tucked in, some with shirts outside. Then, fittingly, last of all, Patsy. Small, and slightly awkward, with neatly parted hair and slightly protruding ears, shoulders back and chest puffed out. His shorts, even in the grainy clip, muddy from the acrobatics of his performance. As he ran through the crowd, a small child jumped into view and reached out with his hand. Patsy Gallacher looked at the young boy, shook his hand and quickly signed his crumpled programme. Then, moments later, passing the camera lens, he was gone. As quickly as he had come. Gone.

The crowd cheered. But there was no sound from the images. The sound of the crowd came from the school hall, an echo of a moment a hundred years before. Everyone was impressed with Robbie's presentation. It had been a success. His mum smiled and clapped proudly. Robbie noticed his mum's smile from the stage, and he was glad that he had given her a reason to smile.

And then he saw. As the proud parents walked away with their children, as the room filled with chatter and laughter, Robbie went to the laptop and looked at the screen as he pulled out his memory stick. The video had paused on the last scene. And standing there looking back from the screen, from Hampden Park. 1925. Frozen in time. His face, his eyes. Unmistakable. It was Fred.

Chapter 42

The Chair

Of course! Robbie thought. The game! Celtic! Hampden Park! Cathkin Park! The handshake! Patsy Gallacher! Everything! Fred had been there. He'd been there too! And now the YouTube clip. That was Fred. It was definitely Fred. Fred and Patsy Gallacher. Robbie was bursting. Like it was the Champions League Final, knowing that he was the one to take the penalty. Stop talking! This is mine! He just knew he had to tell Fred – to see Fred.

Running into the quiet cul-de-sac, he half-expected (and hoped) to see Fred at the front watering the flowers again. But he wasn't.

Robbie rang the old-fashioned doorbell and waited. But the door was already open. Robbie walked through the winding corridor and conservatory, the warm waft of teatime enveloping him. He walked into the lounge. There was a man there playing old-fashioned songs to the residents. Robbie immediately looked at Fred's chair in the corner of the room. But it was empty. Empty like he'd never sat there. Ever. One of the nurses saw Robbie.

'Hi, Robbie!' A carer, who recognised Robbie, came over to him.

'You okay?' she asked kindly.

'I'm fine. Thanks,' Robbie replied confidently enough. 'I've come to see Fred,' he went on.

She looked confused, but in a nice way. 'Fred?'

'Aye, Fred. I need to speak to him. I've found something out. Something important!' Robbie exclaimed, suddenly becoming very animated.

She turned her head towards Robbie and touched his head. She guided Robbie to the corridor. 'Fred's gone, Robbie.'

'What d'you mean, he's gone? Gone where?' Robbie asked anxiously.

'Robbie, he died. He died last week.'

Robbie sucked her words in for a few seconds.

'But he isn't dead! I saw him yesterday. Watering the flowers!'

'No, Robbie. He died last Friday! We tried to tell you yesterday, but you ran off. We couldnae tell you, wee man.'

Robbie knelt down in the communal lounge. His eyes filled up.

'He's dead! But that's impossible! I saw him yesterday! He was watering the flowers! He spoke to me!' Robbie cried out, scrunching his eyes up as they began to fill with tears.

She put her arm around Robbie and hugged him.

'No, Robbie, he died last week. But come, follow me, wee man. He left you something.'

Robbie followed her out of the lounge and into Fred's room. It felt strange. Sitting on Fred's neatly-made bed, knowing that he had died there. Robbie looked around for pictures of his family, but he couldn't see any. There was one picture of a woman. It looked like it was from the 1950s.

A couple of minutes later the nurse returned with a parcel. Written on it were the words: *For Robbie.*

The nurse looked at him and smiled kindly.

'He loved you visiting, Robbie. He lived for you visiting. He often talked about you. He said you'll be a famous footballer one day.'

Robbie opened up the envelope. Inside was a programme. From the Scottish Cup Final 1925. The Patsy Gallacher Final. And it was signed, too.

Dear Fred
It's Never Over!
Patsy

Chapter 43

Almost There!

After Maths, Mr McDougal asked Robbie, Hamish and Jamie to stay back.

'Guys and girls, they have announced the venue for the semi-final – Holm Park! Good, eh? You're home! Luck of the draw, eh?'

'Aye, that's great, Mr McDougal! Maybe it's fate!' Hamish said.

'Aye, maybe, Hamish. But we've still got work to do,' said Mr McDougal, shuffling pieces of paper on his desk.

Robbie nodded, taking it all in.

'Aye, well, I'll see you all at training Thursday?'

'Aye, Mr McDougal,' said Jamie.

With that, the children drifted away from his desk.

'Robbie. How's your fitness?'

'I'm good, Mr McDougal. I feel good,' Robbie replied, giving Mr McDougal the thumbs up as he walked away.

'Good,' Mr McDougal repeated while leaning back into his chair and looking away into the distance, a thin trace of a smile beginning to form on his lips.

The day of the semi-final couldn't come soon enough for Robbie. Apart from training on Thursday, Robbie had had, for him, a light week. It began to dawn on him that the months, now years, of training had paid off. He felt fast, he felt strong, he didn't feel he was about to break in two at any time now. His mum still didn't know, but he reckoned if she was there on the touchline, after a while she wouldn't worry too much. Maybe.

His last visit to the hospital confirmed his improvements. Scans don't lie, he said to himself. And it was proof to him that exercise, his training, his desire to be as strong, as fast and as skilful as anyone in history had come good. Sure, the medicine helped, but he only had to look at poor Fraser to know that it wasn't enough. Not by a long shot.

Before the kick-off, Robbie looked at the opposition: Inverness. They looked big and strong, Robbie thought.

'They look big,' Hamish whispered to Robbie as they warmed up on their side of the pitch.

'Aye. Maybe. But they look slow. And they might be big. But are they strong?'

I'm stronger, Robbie thought. I'm stronger.

Despite Robbie Blair's dismissive analysis, Inverness were actually quite effective. Though they did look a little 'beefy', they did have some speedy players too – and while they provided quite a resolute, steely, defensive back line, they were quick on the counter-attack and had obviously been well drilled in getting the ball up quickly to their pacey forward line. Clydebank really should have gone behind, and would have done had it not been for some goalkeeping heroics from Callum and a goal line clearance from Jamie. Robbie himself just hadn't got into the game at all, much to his frustration.

Early in the second half, Inverness came flooding forward again. Their two pacey attackers exchanged passes and then the taller of them, a blond-haired lad, unleashed a fearsome shot which seemed to hang in the air for an eternity. Clydebank held its breath, but at the last moment the ball hit the bar.

Callum took a goal kick and passed it short to the left back. The left back quickly played it to Hamish in the middle. Hamish took a touch and, after working out who was available, hopped it over the top to Robbie. Robbie was already in full flight and, after seeing the ball hovering over him, stretched with the outside of his left foot and cushioned it in mid-air. Robbie had never done this before and the skill brought cheers from the crowd, from both sides.

The Inverness goalkeeper came to Robbie. Robbie looked up and, judging the angle too tight to score, held back. Out of nowhere, he then decided to rainbow flick the keeper, rolling the ball up the back of his left leg and tossing it over the hapless keeper's head. Now through, Robbie drew back his leg and prepared to pull the trigger. But he didn't.

One of the burly defenders had actually managed to get back in time and made it into the goalmouth, defending the entrance to the goal. Luckily, Jamie had followed Robbie's run and was waiting in the middle. A simple pass from Robbie and then Jamie passed it into the corner.

1-0. Would there even be time for the restart?

Clydebank had done it. They were in the final.

When Robbie got home that night, he sneaked open the front door and saw his mum watching a film in the lounge. He was used to sneaking out of the house. How hard could it be sneaking in?

'Where've you been?' she shouted.

'Nowhere,' Robbie said unconvincingly.

'You've been playing football. In a game!' she said suddenly in Robbie's face, out of nowhere. 'Don't even try and lie to me. I've been texted by five people already!'

'Cos I knew what you'd say!'

Crying, Robbie Blair's mum swallowed him up in her arms.

'Why didn't you tell me you'd got so good?!'

Chapter 44

The Teacher

Rat-a-tat-tat went the letterbox. The Blairs did have a doorbell but whoever was there was in too much of a rush to use it. Robbie got up from the sofa and peered through the letterbox. His mum had already left for the factory and Robbie was under strict instructions not to open the door to any strangers. All he could see were legs, and then suddenly his face met with a face. It was a face he knew: Mr McDougal.

'Is your maw in?'

'She's gone to work. Why?'

'I need to speak to you both.'

'Well, she's not here.'

'Look, Robbie, I shouldnae do this. Could you let me in? I need to speak to you. It's important.'

'Well, okay.' Robbie slipped the latch and opened the door.

'Robbie.' Mr McDougal sat on the sofa. His eyes were alive. They seemed to pierce though Robbie. Robbie wasn't that keen on being pierced, and looked away.

'Are you okay? Are you feeling all right?' Mr McDougal pointed his finger and then lifted his other hand. Both hands pointed to the ceiling. He was dressed in running gear. Robbie had noticed him running around, and had also noticed he seemed to have lost weight. His fingers were still suspended, pointing in the air. Robbie was still looking.

Mr McDougal suddenly got up and started pacing around Robbie Blair's lounge. Robbie followed him around with his eyes.

'I get it,' Mr McDougal said eventually.

'Get what?'

'I get you and I get your dreams. I get your sleepwalking – running – I get your skill and I get your determination. I get Patsy Gallacher. I get all of it. You're not going mad. You're not mad. You're just determined.'

Robbie wasn't sure what to say, so he said, 'Okay.'

'You know when I found you by the Titan that night, you didn't know who I was, remember? You were talking about Patsy Gallacher and rivets and I walked you back. Remember?'

'Aye.' Then Robbie thought. 'No.' Then he thought again. 'Maybe.'

'Maybe I thought you'd gone mad. Maybe I thought you talked to dead people!' Mr McDougal continued.

'That's nice. Thanks.'

Mr McDougal chuckled to himself. And, for a moment, Robbie thought he was talking to his dad. His dad used to chuckle like that. His dad wasn't always bad.

'Robbie! Every time you've seen Patsy Gallacher, perhaps you've been speaking to yourself? Don't you see? Patsy Gallacher was a small, puny player destined to do nothing on a football pitch. But he broke the mould. He broke his leg too, and went on to be one of the best players that's ever been. And he was different to every player that's been. Every time you see his face, that's you. You are Patsy Gallacher!'

Robbie looked uncomfortable. 'Now you're just freakin' me out.'

'No. You're not getting what I'm saying. Patsy Gallacher's become the face for how you were going to overcome all the disappointments and setbacks in your life. Every time you see Patsy Gallacher's face, that's your face. That's how strong you could be. That's how fast you could be. That's how good you could be. And the reason you've been training at night – well, I'm not a psychiatrist but maybe your maw needs to let you off the lead!'

Mr McDougal stood there with his words. 'Are ye with me?'

Robbie looked at him. 'Aye. Maybe.'

Mr McDougal continued. 'But remember. This is your story, Robbie. Your story is about bones. Not ghosts.'

Chapter 45

The Meeting

There was a week to go. To Robbie Blair, there was a year to go. That's what it felt like. Literally. A week to go to the final. It was like his whole life was leading to this game. He could think of nothing else, so was in dire need of something to take his mind off it. A distraction. Something other than lessons.

Mr McDougal provided the answer.

'Right, children. Again, something different for you today! As part of our local history project, we are going to the home of Scottish football: Hampden Park. Now, who has been to Hampden before?'

About ten children put their hands up. Not exactly a sea of hands, Robbie thought, considering that they were only fourteen miles from the hallowed turf. And Robbie was one of those who didn't put up a hand. Why hadn't he been? Money, he supposed. Only maw and him. He could kind of see it. And dad? The ones with their hands up – I bet their dads took them, he thought.

The bus was waiting outside. Oh, the excitement! Robbie, turning everything to football, imagined it was Scottish Cup Final day and he was taking the open-top team bus to Hampden. Robbie wondered how Patsy Gallacher would have felt on cup final day, on the day he scored *that*

Goal. Robbie sat by Hamish, as always halfway up the bus. Instinctively, he always sat halfway. Can keep an eye on everything from halfway. Survey the pitch. Know what's gone, what's coming. Naughty, loud kids at the back, nerds at the front, talking to the teachers. All-rounders in the middle. Robbie would sit here when he was older. On a different bus, but in the same place.

The bus pulled into Hampden Park and a guide was there to meet the class. His name was Bruce. Bruce was a grey-haired, jolly fellow with a beard, in his 60s, Robbie presumed. The tour started in the Scottish Football Museum. Robbie was captivated by it, especially by the displays showing Scottish football from the olden days. The images were black and white, but in a way he saw them in colour. Now.

The changing rooms next. Pristine and shiny. Robbie sat with his arms folded on the bench, absorbing the stillness of the atmosphere and the players who would have sat here, the team talks they would have had, echoing around the tiled room. Bruce was a mine of information. Fact upon fact streamed from his mouth.

Next came the pitch. Anticipation flowed through Robbie's veins as he waited with his class behind the double doors that led to the pitch. Bruce's dramatic words and the soundtrack were not needed for Robbie, as a different soundtrack and commentary played out in his head.

And, with a dramatic flourish, the doors were flown open and the perfect green stage of Hampden Park filled their eyes.

The children all stood by the pitch, either side of the tunnel. Some looked down the tunnel, as if expecting Celtic or Scotland to suddenly appear. But then someone did appear. Robbie didn't see the doors open, but on match days perhaps the doors are always open. Not overly tall and slight. But he looked strong, fit. His mousey hair was curly, unruly, as if it wouldn't be told to be anything but. To Robbie he looked about eighteen. His hooped Celtic shirt hung down over his white shorts. His mouth looked nervous but his eyes looked ready. And his eyes. Robbie recognised them. And he looked into Robbie. Deep and still. One green and one blue.

'How are you?' Robbie said.

Chapter 46

Family

Robbie Blair woke up on Saturday morning knowing this day was going to be different. He knew that even if he lost today, he had still won. Because he was playing football again. He felt strong. Though he was still small, he felt he could pummel into the ground any player he came up against. He felt fast. Eighteen months of swimming pool drills, gym workouts and running between lamp posts and up hills had made him into somebody different. And he was more skilful than before. Months of dreaming up skills and executing them with a tennis ball with every moment of every day.

When Robbie was eating his cornflakes in the front room, his mum came over to speak to him.

'Robbie?'

'Aye?'

'I know about Fred.'

Robbie said nothing, but stopped eating. He looked blankly into the television screen.

'But, Robbie. I've found something out.' For a change, Mrs Blair seemed totally focused on what she was saying. Nothing else mattered.

'Gina, my sister, has been in touch. She's been doing a family history project since she got made redundant from the factory.'

Robbie turned around to look at her, sensing something.

'Robbie. She's found out that Fred is family. He's your great-great-uncle. Your great-granddad's brother. We never realised. No one realised he had family. He was forgotten by everyone. Except you.'

It was too much for Robbie, and he rushed upstairs. He climbed into bed with his letter and his old football shirt and cried. That old shirt that he had never shown anyone, that Robbie kept hidden away, like his dreams.

When he stopped crying, Robbie thought about Fred. Patsy Gallacher was Fred's childhood hero and that moment in Hampden Park, all those years ago, was as fresh in his eyes as an old man as when it had happened in 1925. Every time he told him stories about Patsy Gallacher, it was if it was happening now, again, right before Robbie's eyes. Like they were his memories too.

Chapter 47

The Final – Part 1

Earlier in the week, when Robbie had been told where the final was going to be, he couldn't believe it.

Mr McDougal took him to one side after assembly.

'Cathkin Park, Robbie! The former home of Scottish football!'

'Aye, that's great, Mr McDougal.' Robbie felt a wave of excitement inside him but also a steely feeling, like everything was clicking into place. And back to Cathkin Park – Robbie couldn't have picked a more perfect place.

On the day of the final, Robbie's mum went off to work and called out to him.

'I'll see you later, love. We'll take the train.'

'Aye,' Robbie replied. It's too far to run, he thought. Much too far.

When they arrived at Crosshill, Robbie just wanted to start the game. He was properly nervous now. As they headed down to Cathkin Park, he saw the curtain of trees that shielded the pitch from the outside world and thought to himself, I am finally here.

There was a rumour that one of the Celtic coaches would be at the game, and when Mr McDougal was pressed on this he answered cagily, 'Aye, maybe.'

During the warm-up, Robbie noticed that one of their defenders was Kyle Ferguson. He knew Kyle had moved from the area and so didn't expect their paths to be crossing again so soon. Even the way he was stretching, kicking out his leg like he was some kind of pro, annoyed Robbie.

Jamie whispered, 'Oh, look who it is! Well, never mind, Robbie, you just concentrate on your own game. Just you see.'

Her comforting words halted Robbie's gaze and he shrugged, 'Aye, you're right.'

When the referee blew the whistle, Robbie suddenly thought of the shipyard whistle signalling the end of the shift, of the whistle that Fred had talked about that signalled the time to go. This was Robbie's time to go. Action. In contrast to the semi-final, Clydebank started strongly this time. Wave after wave, attack after attack. Robbie was on fire: fast, strong and orchestrating everything from his wing, always going forward and always waiting to cut in and attack. Energy coursed through his legs, giving him confidence to explode past defenders with ease.

Paisley somehow managed to cling on and keep it to 0-0 at the break.

Mr McDougal gathered the team around him. 'Simple. Don't change a thing. It will come. It will come.'

With an hour gone, some of Clydebank were wondering whether it would ever come. But Robbie didn't panic, and the driving bass and drums that he had felt two years before started to course through his body. It was coming. Faint at first and then stronger, stronger. On one of the terraces in the trees, by himself, an old man stood and watched. Robbie saw him.

The ball came to Robbie and he was gone. Past the first defender in a flash and then on past the next. Daylight. Then, in his sights, the keeper. Robbie drew back his leg and pretended to shoot but then dropped his shoulder and went to the keeper's right. He was too quick for the keeper now, who had already committed to the dive to his left, bringing Robbie down. Penalty.

Mr McDougal shouted out. 'Let Robbie have it!'

Robbie looked at the keeper more intently than he had ever looked at anything in his life. His green and blue eyes unwavering, lost in the moment. The moment seemed to last an eternity, but it was just a moment to everyone else. He waited for the keeper to move to the right and then passed it down into the empty net, straight down the centre. 1-0.

A sloppy defensive error led to Paisley equalising. Clydebank gave away the ball needlessly in their own half and one of their pacey wingers capitalised, running through and skilfully placing the ball into the bottom corner.

Then the ball was launched over the defenders, all eyes to the sky. This was it.

Robbie grabbed the ball, cushioned it in the air with the outside of his foot and readied himself to score. He was just outside the six-yard box. Suddenly, as before, like a train, Kyle Ferguson came out of nowhere and bulldozed him to the floor. It was if the last two years had been bulldozed too. Robbie felt the pain again and lay lifeless on the floor. His teammates stood over him.

Chapter 48

The Final – Part 2

Robbie lay there, listless, dazed in the mud. Like he was in hospital, but it was as if things were happening to somebody else, not him. Then he heard the voice. But he wasn't sure this time where the voice came from. Robbie saw Patsy, then Fred, then Ryan, then Mr McDougal. Then himself.

'Jump!' they said. And so he did. Feeling the ball between his boots, Robbie clambered to his feet and then, crouching slightly, braced himself for the inevitable. Breathing one last gasp of air in, eyes fixed on the prize, he launched himself through the air and over the keeper into the net. And that was that.

But if it was just a that, it was a big that.

The referee blew. And the seagulls circled and swooped. But they watched.

Robbie lay in the goalmouth, his boots entangled in the net, not quite aware of what had just happened. Squinting into the sunlight, he recognised the face that stared down over him. Jamie. She was smiling.

'You did it, Robbie! We've won. I've never seen anything like it. Are you okay? You've nae broken anything, have you?'

Untangling his boots from the net, Robbie waved his legs in the air as he lay on the turf.

'No, I'm all good,' he replied, smiling.

Jamie helped him to his feet and they both walked across the pitch to their jubilant teammates. As he walked across the familiar turf, he stopped and gazed at the watching trees that looked down from the terraces. And there, standing on the concrete steps, little legs, Celtic scarf dangling down, almost touching the ground, gazing out onto the pitch, he saw himself with his dad. Of course! This was the park! This is where he had come with his dad – when he was five.

'Are you okay, Robbie?' Jamie asked softly.

'Aye,' said Robbie. 'I've just remembered something, that's all. Something I've got to do.'

When they reached the others, Robbie was lifted up by the team and carried off the pitch. Again. This time not as a casualty, but as a hero.

Mr McDougal came over to Robbie, shaking his head, smiling. Mr McDougal looked at him intently. He was a tall man but he wasn't looking *down* at him, just at him. They were the same.

'Well done, Robbie. You did it. You did it. And did you know there was someone from Celtic coming to watch you today?'

'No,' Robbie replied, still out of breath.

'Aye, Robbie, he was in the stands. He liked what he saw.'

'Well, that's good,' Robbie replied. 'I cannae believe it's all happened, Mr McDougal. But in a way I dunnae know how it's happened. Is it all a dream?'

'You cannae explain everything, Robbie. Not everything can be explained. That's just the way it is. You're good at running, aren't you?'

'Aye, now I am.'

'Well, run with that, then, Robbie. Run with that.'

Epilogue

Seven years later

Celtic…Celtic…Celtic…Celtic.
Come on you bhoys in green.
Come on you bhoys in green.
Glasgow's green and white.
Glasgow's green and white.

Making his way down the corridors from the changing rooms, Robbie heard the familiar chants of Parkhead echoing down the Hampden tunnel. The call and response of 'Come on the bhoys in green', which was thrown back and forth across the stadium from the rooftops like a football being tossed around by tempestuous waves, echoing through the tunnel and up the stairs, bouncing off the white-tiled walls. As they got nearer and nearer, the sound became louder, like an old radio being tuned in, finding the right frequency, and then suddenly – the perfect spot.

As the team waited in the tunnel, Robbie thought for a moment. This was it. All the breaks. The hospital. The medicine. The running. The training. Fred. Patsy Gallacher. Mr McDougal. Jamie. Ryan. The dreams. It had all led here. And that was the point. Here. Now.

*

Hail! Hail! The Celts are here!
Oh what the hell do we care?
What the hell do we care?

Hail! Hail! The Celts are here!
Oh what the hell do we care now?

And now the team stood in the tunnel. Robbie stood, halfway along the line. Players in front and players behind, just the way he liked it. Three players down from him, the keeper towered over everyone, and then in front of him the shaven-headed captain stood – eyes fixed, braced – unmoving.

And then it happened. As the door opened.

And as the crowd roared.

Robbie stood. And looked.

The End
By JG Nolan

Patsy Gallacher
October '21
DLG

Cathkin Park

As you have seen in the beautiful and evocative illustrations by Carina Roberts throughout this book, Cathkin Park plays an important part in Robbie Blair's story.

You could even say that Cathkin Park is the spiritual home of *Jump!*

For actor Simon Weir, the connection with Cathkin Park is just as strong, with his great grandfather playing at the ground for Third Lanark, one of the proud founding fathers of the Scottish game. Sadly, Third Lanark was liquidated, and their membership of the Scottish Football League removed in 1967.

Cathkin Park then fell into disrepair and most of the fabric was gradually removed – although the pitch and some of the terraces are still there, peeking out through the greenery. According to the volunteers who have been diligently working to restore the Park, it still smells and looks like a football ground!

The restoration work has been spearheaded by Simon, who in moments of rest from clearing weeds from the crumbling terraces, can imagine his great grandfather on the pitch, hear the crowds roar and smell the smoke from their pipes.

If you would like to follow Simon's journey in bringing Cathkin Park back to life please follow @CathkinPark on Twitter.

Lightning Source UK Ltd.
Milton Keynes UK
UKHW052008300622
405196UK00006B/240